Somebody's Girl

ORCA YOUNG READERS

Somebody's Girl

Maggie de Vries

[redacted]

ORCA BOOK PUBLISHERS

Library and Archives Canada Cataloguing in Publication

De Vries, Maggie
Somebody's girl / Maggie de Vries.
(Orca young readers)

Issued also in electronic format.
ISBN 978-1-55469-383-2

I. Title. II. Series: Orca young readers
PS8557.E895S64 2011 JC813'.54 C2010-907920-5

First published in the United States, 2011
Library of Congress Control Number: 2010941923

Summary: Martha knows she is adopted, but when her mother becomes pregnant, she worries about no longer being number one in her parents' hearts.

Mixed Sources
Product group from well-managed forests, controlled sources and recycled wood or fiber
www.fsc.org Cert no. SW-COC-000952
© 1996 Forest Stewardship Council
FSC

Orca Book Publishers is dedicated to preserving the environment and has printed this book on paper certified by the Forest Stewardship Council.

Orca Book Publishers gratefully acknowledges the support for its publishing programs provided by the following agencies: the Government of Canada through the Canada Book Fund and the Canada Council for the Arts, and the Province of British Columbia through the BC Arts Council and the Book Publishing Tax Credit.

Typesetting by Jasmine Devonshire
Cover artwork by Suzanne Duranceau
Author photo by Roland Kokke

ORCA BOOK PUBLISHERS
PO Box 5626, Stn. B
Victoria, BC Canada
V8R 6S4

ORCA BOOK PUBLISHERS
PO Box 468
Custer, WA USA
98240-0468

www.orcabook.com
Printed and bound in Canada.

14 13 12 11 • 4 3 2 1

To Clea, Dea, Kathryn and Tanya: friends for life.

Contents

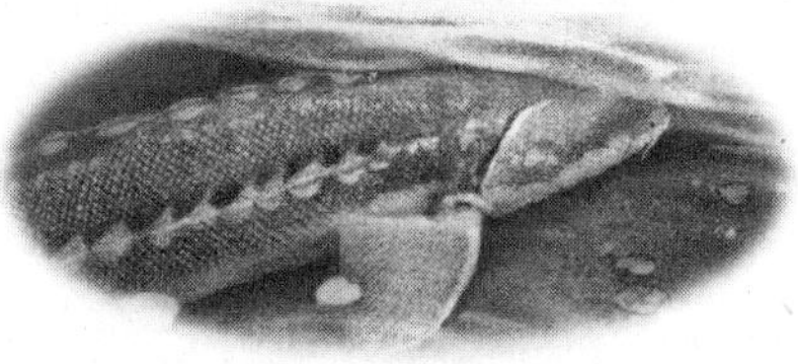

CHAPTER 1

A Girl, a Boy and a Great Big Fish

"Hailey, you'll be partners with Emily," Mr. Jewett said. "And Martha—"

Martha had trouble lifting her eyes from the back page of her notebook.

Martha Serena Johnson.

Martha Serena Johnson.

Martha Serena Johnson.

Her name looked lovely lined up like that, the letters all swirly. She was developing beautiful handwriting, if she did say so herself. She loved the last two parts of her name, but she would never understand why Mom and Dad had let her birth mother give her any name at all, let alone such a plain-Jane name as Martha.

"Martha," the teacher said again, "you'll be partners with Chance."

Martha flinched. To be stuck with a boy was bad enough. She was sure almost all the other pairs were boy/boy and girl/girl. But to be stuck with Chance?

Ever since Chance had shown up in Martha's class last spring, all jumpy and annoying, and always, always in trouble, Martha had kept her distance. He was a foster child—everyone knew it. Martha was adopted, which was a whole different thing. She wished she could get up in front of the whole school and tell them. And she wished that nobody—nobody—knew. Now Mr. Jewett was pairing up the adopted girl and the fostered boy, like they belonged together. But Chance was nothing like her. Nothing at all.

Yes, Chance had settled down a bit since last year. They were three weeks into grade four, and he hadn't hit anyone yet, at least not that Martha had seen. Most days he was lined up outside with everyone else at the end of lunch and recess, instead of slinking back to class from the principal's office.

In addition to being messed up in every other way, Chance couldn't even do his five times tables. In grade four! And he couldn't tell time from the clock on the wall. He had to look at his digital watch. Martha had noticed.

Besides, he had a friend. Ken, that boy from Hong Kong, was always hanging around with him. Why couldn't Chance and Ken be partners?

"Why can't I be partners with Ken?" said Chance.

Martha flinched again. She could not believe that Chance had dared to ask when she had not. She glanced across the room, met Preeti's eyes and longed for things to be the way they were last year, when at least she had had friends. Preeti looked away. Well, Martha knew she had ruined that friendship herself.

"No, Chance. You will be working with Martha, and Ken will be working with Jonas." Mr. Jewett raised a hand when Chance opened his mouth to speak again. "I have my reasons," he said, smiling as he said it.

Martha wasn't smiling. She thought she knew exactly what those reasons were, and they weren't right. She narrowed her eyes as Chance approached her desk, thumping his chair along the floor behind him. How dared he ask for a different partner?

He narrowed his eyes right back, but she looked down at her work.

Sturgeon spawn every twelve years, she wrote in her neatest cursive, with a lovely flourish on each *y*.

"Do you know what *spawn* means?"

Martha's head jerked up as Chance spoke, much too close to her ear.

"Of course I do!"

"Babies," Chance said, looking right into her eyes. "It means having babies." He paused. "Like your mom."

Martha clenched her right hand into a fist.

"My mother is not *spawning*," she said, keeping her voice low. "My mother is having a baby. Only fish spawn."

"That's not true," Chance said. "Frogs spawn. And toads." He thought for a moment. "So do salamanders and newts."

Martha dug her nails into her palm and imagined her fist connecting with Chance's nose. She glanced toward Mr. Jewett's desk and met the teacher's eyes. He drew his brows together and gave his head a small shake. How did he know what she was thinking? Well, she wouldn't have punched Chance in class anyway. Or in her new outfit.

Martha swished her long dark hair across her back, feeling its comforting weight, and turned her attention back to her worksheet. *How much would a ninety-year-old sturgeon weigh?* She would have to consult that weird sturgeon age-and-weight chart to work it out. Chance would be no help. Who cared about the weight of a great, big, stupid garbage-sucking fish anyway? She tried to ignore the heat in her face and the pounding in her chest.

If only her mother and Chance's foster mother, Angie, weren't best friends.

Martha's class had been studying sturgeon since the first day of grade four. Martha already knew how boring the fish were. September was going to be over soon. Maybe, she dared to hope, the big-fish project would be over soon too.

"Class," Mr. Jewett said, "you're all settled with your new partners now. Your new partnership is very, very important. You see, you are going to be working together on the sturgeon project for some time."

Martha could not believe what she was hearing.

A rumble of mumbles greeted Mr. Jewett, but he just waved his arm in the air. "For today, I'd like you to complete your worksheets together. Help each other. Share your knowledge. And get to know each other a little bit."

The mumbles settled down in the face of an easy task.

Martha glanced at Chance's worksheet. It looked as if it had been attacked by a pack of starving gerbils. Or maybe a sturgeon had spawned on it. Or a newt.

Then something else occurred to her. Chance might be lacking in brains, and he might be messy, but he did know a thing or two about fish.

"So, partner," she said, "how much would a ninety-year-old sturgeon weigh?"

By the time the bell went, her worksheet was finished, and she suspected that every answer was right too. She had not liked writing Chance's name under hers at the top, but Mr. Jewett had insisted they combine their work, and Chance had given her almost all the answers.

He didn't seem to have too much trouble with numbers if they related to the weight, length or girth of a fish.

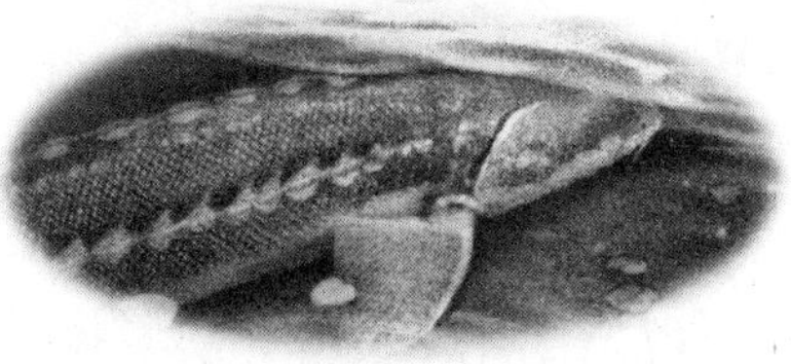

CHAPTER 2

Mom Lies Down

Martha's mom looked up from where she stood at the kitchen counter peeling carrots for Martha's lunch. She frowned.

"That's not the outfit I put out for you, Martha. That skirt and top don't match." Her voice rose, just a little. "And I'm sure that T-shirt was at the bottom of the stack." She dropped the peeler, gave her hands a wipe on the dishcloth and strode past Martha toward Martha's room.

"I took it out carefully," Martha said as she chased her mother up the stairs. "Why can't I wear what I want?"

Mom stood in the bedroom doorway. Martha stepped up behind her. The cupboard door was open, but the stack of shirts was all folded back into place. Her nightie was in the hamper. She had even given the duvet a shake and pulled it up like Mom always asked her to.

Mom sighed. "I'll tidy up here later," she said. "I haven't finished making your lunch, and I have a doctor's appointment this morning. Why can't you just wear what I lay out?" She reached into the closet. "Here's the shirt I picked for you. Change." And she was gone, back to the kitchen.

Martha resisted stomping her foot. Her mother had picked out a purple shirt to go with the purple and gray skirt that Martha had on. Martha looked down at the yellow shirt that she had selected herself. She knew it went with the skirt. She just did. Look at me, it called out. I look good.

She pulled off the yellow shirt and tossed it on her bed. The other one was pretty, and the outfit worked. But in it, she was just another boring girl. All matchy-matchy.

What had Linda, her birth mother, worn when she was nine? Martha wondered. She'd be willing to bet that Linda had not limited herself to purple with purple and pink with pink. She gave her head a shake. Why was she even thinking about her birth mother?

Linda had only just started seeing Martha again last Christmas after being gone for more than two years. Martha was better off choosing her own clothes.

In Martha's opinion, open adoptions just created problems. Her birth mother had given her away, but she still got to give her a name. She still got to see her if she wanted, but then she could disappear for years too. "She has problems," Mom had explained more than once. "She wants to see you. She really does. But she struggles. She has trouble finding work and holding down a job."

Those were just excuses as far as Martha was concerned. Not that she wanted to see Linda anyway. And when she and Mom and Dad had gone out for dinner with Linda just before Christmas last year, Martha had backed away from the pale bony woman with stringy black hair who breathed smoker's breath on her when she tried to hug her. Since then, she had seen Linda four more times: three times with Mom and once with Mom and Dad. Linda was looking a little fatter the last time, in July, when they had gone to an outdoor pool together, but she still smelled of smoke. And she still had a kind of desperate way about her when she came at Martha for one of those hugs.

Martha looked at herself in the mirror, smoothed down the front of her skirt and pulled her hair around over her shoulder. It might be black like Linda's, and long like Linda's too, but it was thick and glossy and neatly trimmed every few weeks by her mom's hairdresser, Quentina.

She was due for a trim soon, actually, but she wouldn't have to see Linda again for at least another month. Martha slid her feet into her shoes, grabbed her bag, ran downstairs and set off for school.

Chance and Martha were in the computer lab doing research on sturgeon. They had found the Fraser River Sturgeon Conservation Society website.

"*...novel life history and migration information for the species...*" Martha read off the monitor.

"That doesn't make any sense," Chance said.

"Yes, it does," Martha said. "It means..." She hated to admit that she didn't get it either.

"Angie says your mom's not doing so well," Chance said.

Martha's head snapped around. "Why are you talking with Angie about my mom?"

Chance's face sort of collapsed. "I...I didn't..."

"You didn't what? My mother is just fine, thank you."

Chance looked mad all of a sudden. "Okay," he said. "If that's the way you want it. Your *mother* is just fine."

Martha saw the red flush across his neck and chin. How dared he say *mother* like that? She met his eyes. "At least my parents adopted me," she said clearly. "You're just a foster kid. You and that whiny little Louise. Mark's the only real kid in *your* family."

She watched Chance closely as she said it. The skin across his cheeks tightened and grew pale. Martha's stomach flipped.

Mark was two years older, in grade six. Last year, when Chance had come along, Mark had been furious, Martha remembered. He had thought that one foster child—that sobbing baby, Louise—had been more than enough. He was Angie and Doug's biological son, not adopted, not a foster child. Martha had never liked him, but she sympathized. Imagine living with Chance!

"And I see my real mother all the time," she added, squirming a little inside as she said it. Linda was her birth mother, yes, but not her *real* mother. Not really. And Martha had been seeing her regularly for less than a year. And not liking one minute of it.

Chance was not looking at her anymore. He was staring at the computer screen, as if concentration could unlock the words there and release their meanings.

"I don't remember my real mother," he said, his voice almost too quiet to hear.

"Well, I know mine," she said, a little too loudly.

Chance looked up at her. "I'm going back to class," he said, shoving his chair back. It started to tip, and Martha righted it. Chance bumped his hip against a book display on his way out, and books cascaded to the floor.

Ms. Barnston looked up from her desk. "Chance," she called after him, "pick those up." But he was gone.

Ignoring her racing heart, Martha turned back to the computer and shut it down.

As Martha collected her papers and pushed in the chairs, Ms. Barnston looked up from the floor, where she was gathering up the fallen books. She watched Martha for a moment and then held out one of the books she had just picked up.

Martha looked at the cover. Hilary McKay. *Forever Rose*.

"It's been a while since you took out a book, Martha," Ms. Barnston said as she used a table edge to heave herself to her feet. "This one is brand-new!"

Martha shook her head sharply. "I'm okay, Ms. Barnston," she said. "I have to go back to class." And she marched out of the library, clutching the papers tight to her chest. Those were not tears in her eyes. They were not.

"I want to do the oldest fish," Chance called out.

"Hang on, Chance," Mr. Jewett said. "A couple of other kids actually had their hands up."

Martha was not one of them, but she was glad to see Mr. Jewett wasn't letting Chance break all the rules. Moments later, the conversation circled back to Chance's request.

"The oldest sturgeons are more than six meters long," Mr. Jewett said. "Do you have any idea how big that is?"

Out came a long ruler. Mr. Jewett had children take turns, marking each length off with a bit of tape. Martha bent over her math sheet. In her mind, though, the fish grew and grew and grew. It turned out that the two-hundred-year-old creature would barely fit in their classroom. Could such a monster exist?

"I'm afraid we can't make a fish that big," Mr. Jewett said. "Chance, you and Martha can make the biggest one we're doing, since you asked first." He seemed to have forgotten that Chance hadn't put up his hand.

The class was going to make fifteen fish, starting with larvae and ending with a ninety-year-old (or middle-aged) sturgeon. Mr. Jewett wrote names on the chart on the wall. Martha watched as he wrote her name down next to Chance's beside the words *ninety-year-old, four-meter-long fish.* She felt a flutter of excitement.

Mr. Jewett had wheeled in a stand holding an enormous roll of brown paper. The larvae and young-of-the-year pairs only needed regular sheets of paper, but since sturgeon grew fast, everyone else got part of the roll. When it came time to roll out paper for the ninety-year-old fish, Martha loved how the whole class gasped when one meter, two meters, three meters and a fourth meter spread across the floor. Chance and Martha took turns measuring and marking. When they were done, Mr. Jewett asked Martha to tear the sheet off the roll against the sharp metal edge that held the paper in place. She loved the cool smoothness of the paper, the ripping sound and the clean straight edge that she created.

Then Martha and Chance had to make decisions. Were they going to draw the fish from the side or the top? How could they figure out how tall or how wide the fish would be? Their chart didn't show that information. How were they going to divide up the work?

When Martha walked into the house after school that day, Mom was lying on the couch. Martha felt a small jolt in her middle. Mom rarely even *sat* on the couch, unless they had company. Martha had never seen her *lie* there until two weeks ago. Today was the third time.

"Hi, honey," Mom said, when Martha was standing over her. "How was your day?"

“Fine,” Martha said, watching to see if her mother would get up to fetch her a snack.

Mom showed no signs of moving. Both her hands rested gently on her belly. Martha saw those hands shift slightly, cupping what was inside her, that new baby. Her belly was starting to get bigger, and she was always touching it. When she did, her eyes would stop looking out, and Martha knew that she had gone inside where the baby was. They were hanging out together, mother and baby.

Had her birth mother ever done that? Martha wondered. Stupid question. Linda hadn’t even taken her home for one day before she handed her over to Mom and Dad. She hadn’t wanted her for one second. Mom and Dad had told her many times that Linda had given Martha to them out of love. That she didn’t have a good home for her, that she wasn’t well. Martha knew better. If Linda had really, really loved her, she would never have given her away.

“I’ll get my own snack,” Martha said, keeping her voice smooth. “You rest.”

“All right,” Mom said. Martha was halfway to the kitchen when her mother added, “Sweetheart, do you think you could fetch me a glass of milk?

I'm supposed to drink so much of it, you know, and I keep forgetting."

Martha stopped for the tiniest second. Something cold and dreadful ran through her body. Her mother had never asked to be waited on before. She turned her head. "Okay, Mom," she said.

In the kitchen doorway she stopped again, almost stepping on a heap of cloth bags. One last bag lay collapsed on the counter surrounded by jars and cans. Martha had never seen the kitchen like this unless Mom was standing there, putting the groceries away. She must have put the eggs and meat in the fridge and gone straightaway to lie down.

Martha opened the cupboard to get a glass, but the shelf was empty. She stared for a moment, thinking. The dishwasher. Her mom hadn't even unloaded the dishwasher. Clean glass retrieved, she poured a glass of milk and took it into the living room. As she set it on the coffee table, her mother held out her hand.

"Honey, just put it right here," Mom said. "That way I don't have to sit up."

Martha did what she asked and headed for the stairs. She wasn't hungry anymore.

In her room, with the door closed behind her, she took one long look at the bookshelf between the windows. The books gleamed in familiar colorful rows. Last year, she had read to herself every night before supper and before bed. She had learned to read real chapter books by then, and she had loved how black marks on a page could carry her away to a whole other place. Reading had seemed like a miracle.

The books still looked pretty, but they were solid objects now, as if the covers were glued down, the pages stuck together. Nowadays, no matter what Martha did, she seemed to be stuck inside her own real life. She turned away from the shelf and collapsed onto her bed.

Curled up there, with a pillow in her arms, she thought back to grade three. She had come right home from school then, if she didn't have dance class. And she had almost always had friends in tow.

Sam and Hailey and Preeti.

Martha gave her head a shake. She did not want to think about those girls. But the memories pushed their way in anyway.

Last year, Mom always had something special waiting: a banana loaf or squares or cookies from the

Farmers' Market or the Italian Bakery. She would come out of her office to greet the girls and settle them at the kitchen table with tall glasses of juice or milk. Martha's friends all liked Martha's mom. They chattered on about her clothes, her hair, her makeup. They loved it when she commented on Sam's top or Hailey's shoes or Preeti's haircut.

And Martha had loved every minute of it—loved it, that is, until she brought the girls through the kitchen door back in the middle of June. Martha had walked in and stopped short, the others crowding her into the room. Mom was right there at the kitchen table that day, but not in her usual work clothes. She had on a ratty old nightgown without a robe. Martha hadn't even known she owned such a thing. And her hair looked like she had just crawled out of bed.

When the door opened, Mom had looked up from the table and smiled—no—beamed. Something was strange and different and wrong. If Martha could have, she would have backed right out of the house again, pushing Preeti and Sam and Hailey behind her, but they were already in. They were staring.

Shame flooded through Martha down to her toes. What would they think of her mother, her perfect mother, now? “You have to go,” Martha said fiercely to the three girls. “You have to go right now.”

They were standing in a tight bunch, staring at Martha, not at her mother. “Go?” Preeti said blankly. “But—”

“Just go,” Martha said, hating the way her voice rose, almost to a screech, knowing somewhere inside her that her behavior made no sense. And she pushed them out the door and closed it on them.

By the time she turned around, her mom was standing in the middle of the kitchen. That’s when Martha saw her bare feet, and the big coffee stain on the white flannel of her nightgown.

“Honey,” her mom said, her voice warm with concern—and something else.

How dare her mother talk to her like that when she had embarrassed her in front of her friends, when she was dressed like a crazy person, bare feet even? Martha gave her one look and burst into tears.

“Honey,” Mom said again, “come here.”

Martha took a step away instead. That was when Dad came through the door. He looked from daughter to mother and back again. “Sweetheart,” he said to Martha, “why is there a huddle of girls on the front sidewalk?”

"I...," Martha said. Couldn't he see for himself that everything was wrong?

"I embarrassed her," Mom said. "But I'm so glad that you're both here." She paused, and Martha's dad stepped to her side. Then, "Martha, Peter," she said, "I'm going to have a baby."

Martha watched as her parents turned into one big bubble of happiness. She took another step back. And waited. They hugged and they smiled and they murmured. She waited some more.

At last Dad took his gaze from his wife's face and looked at Martha. "Come here, you," he said. "You're going to have a baby brother." He looked at Mom again. "Or sister," he added, laughing as he spoke.

Martha let herself be pulled right in between the two of them. She swayed along in the joy dance. But it did not feel joyful to her. Not joyful at all.

She had only been five years old when Linda, her birth mom, had said to Mom right in front of her, "Weren't you lucky I came along? You waited till awfully late to start trying to adopt. Maybe you should have given up on pregnancy a bit sooner."

Mom had frowned and hushed her, so Martha had known that what Linda was saying was important.

And that was the last time they saw Linda for years. Martha had memorized Linda's words and puzzled over them ever since. She had found out what pregnancy was. And she had figured out that Mom and Dad had adopted her because Mom couldn't get pregnant.

And now Mom *was* pregnant. She and Dad were going to have a baby of their very own. Mom was going to be this baby's birth mom and real mom both at the same time.

Martha wriggled her way out of the happy huddle. "I have homework," she said as she grabbed her backpack and headed for the stairs.

"Maybe you should call the girls and explain," Mom called after her. "They're not going to understand why you treated them so badly. And they'll be happy to hear the news."

Martha paused on the stairs and lowered her chin. She wasn't phoning anybody. She did not like what was going on in her kitchen. And she did not like the change in her mother either. Her mother always met her and her friends after school in nice clothes. She smiled and chatted. She didn't parade around in a dirty nightgown with wild hair at four o'clock in the afternoon. And she didn't have babies either.

The afternoon's events carved out a hot, dark, scary place inside Martha's chest.

Martha had never invited Preeti or Sam or Hailey to her house again, not in all the months since.

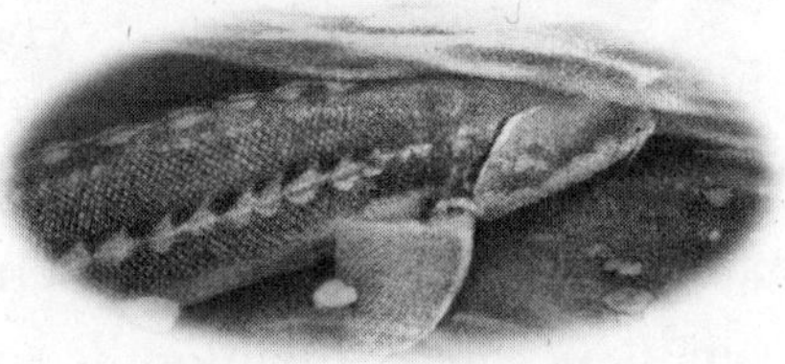

CHAPTER 3

Center of Discovery

Martha was glad they were taking a bus on the field trip. Mom always volunteered to drive when they took cars. She would have hated having her mom there with her belly sticking out.

With a bus, only a few parent volunteers were needed, and Martha's mom did not need to be one of them. Chance's foster dad, Doug, was coming. That was plenty for Martha to deal with.

She was also glad that no one said anything about sitting with their sturgeon partners. She did not want to be stuck with that boy all day. Maybe this was the chance she had been waiting for. The day before the field trip, she cornered Preeti on the schoolground.

"Want to sit with me? On the bus?" she asked, keeping her voice casual.

Preeti appeared to think for a moment. Martha clenched her fists at her sides, out of Preeti's sight.

"Okay," Preeti said. "I guess so."

Martha unclenched her fists. She grinned, but not pathetically, she hoped. "That's great," she said.

Then the bell sent them pelting back to class. Martha ran with joy in her heart.

The bus left first thing the next morning. They would be back at school in time for lunch, and Mr. Jewett was bringing snacks for the whole class.

Martha was putting her books away in her desk when she saw them—Preeti and Sam and Hailey—whispering together at the back of the room. Preeti looked toward her, and Martha pasted on a smile, but Preeti had turned back to the others before Martha's lips were fully in place. More whispers. A laugh. A look from Sam. Then Hailey. Martha recognized the signs. Those girls, who had loved to come to her house every day just a few months ago, were gossiping about her now.

Martha stood still for a moment, leaning on her desk. She had let things go wrong, wrong, wrong. More than once since the day of the dirty nightgown, Mom had suggested that Martha invite her friends over. In July, Dad had suggested a Saturday trip to the water-slides. At each bright idea, Martha had shaken her head while her insides had shriveled up with shame.

They're getting a real baby, she had thought, over and over again. And every sidelong glance or small smile between her parents had confirmed it. At last they had what they wanted. And what, Martha wondered, did that mean for her? If she had to watch Preeti or Hailey or Sam even think that question, she would die. She would fall to the earth that very moment, dead.

And Hailey was sure to do more than think. She would speak the words right into the air. And they could never be taken back.

Martha jumped when the teacher rapped on his desk. "All right, everyone," he said, bringing the excitement under control for the moment. "It's time to get your coats and line up at the door."

Martha had been looking forward to snubbing Chance. She had imagined him approaching her to be his partner on the bus. She would link her arm through Preeti's. "I'm sorry, Chance," she would say (sweetly, ever so sweetly). "Preeti and I are going to sit together."

Now she was hoping that she wasn't about to get snubbed herself. She barely saw Chance barrel into line with Ken.

Please, Preeti, she thought. Please. You promised.

She got up, collected her coat from its hook and wandered toward the line. Preeti was still chatting with Sam and Hailey. At least there were three of them. If they made an even number, Martha would never have stood a chance of getting Preeti to sit with her.

"Come on, girls," Mr. Jewett said. "The bus is leaving."

Martha watched Preeti tear herself away from the other two. Without speaking, she joined Martha in line. Sam and Hailey bustled up right behind them.

"Preeti," Sam said, her voice loud enough to be heard by the whole class, "want to come over to my place after school? Hailey's coming."

"Sure," Preeti said. "I'd love to."

The line started moving then, and the conversation stopped, but it had been enough. If Martha could have crumbled into dust right then and there, she would have.

Face firmly pointed forward, shoulders back, Martha marched out of the school, up the steps and onto the bus. She heard the teasing giggles of the girls behind her, but she tried to shut out the sound. Preeti slid into a window seat and twisted herself to talk to Sam and Hailey, who had taken the row behind them. Martha perched at the edge of the seat beside Preeti. The conversation between the three girls shot right through her. Like dozens of tiny arrows, she thought. She had been crazy, asking to sit with Preeti. She craned her neck to look to the back of the bus, but there was not a spare seat to be had.

Mr. Jewett repeated his instructions, the driver started the engine and the journey began.

The bus had not even left the school parking lot when Preeti spoke. "Hey, Martha," she said, "how come you were so mean to us that day? And why don't you invite us over anymore? We didn't do anything to you."

Horror welled like vomit right up into Martha's throat. She swallowed hard, and for a moment she considered running. Empty seats or no, she could just dart to the back and curl up in a corner.

How could Preeti ask her to spell it all out? And right there on a bus, with everyone listening in?

Martha took a breath and spoke. "I...I...It's not the same at home anymore," she said, knowing that her explanation wasn't enough.

Hailey's voice rang out for everyone to hear. "What, because your mom's pregnant?"

Now it wasn't horror in her throat. It was shame. "No," she blurted, and shrank back in her seat as she realized her voice had traveled the full length of the bus.

Pregnant. How she hated that word.

"Girls. Is something wrong here?"

Martha swallowed hard and leaned out into the aisle. Chance's foster father faced her from several rows back. She shook her head hard at him and looked away just as the bus turned from the parking lot onto the road.

Sam and Hailey had gone silent, and Preeti was glaring at her. "When I agreed to be your bus partner, I didn't realize you'd be getting us into trouble with parents," she hissed.

"I...I didn't mean..." But Martha was speaking to Preeti's back.

This couldn't be happening. Why did Doug have to interfere? Martha didn't know him very well. Angie usually dropped by to visit Martha's mom on her own or with baby Louise in tow. When Martha had seen Doug before, she had always kind of liked him.

Not anymore.

Once they had reached their destination and filed inside, Chance did not give Martha a moment's peace.

As soon as Mr. Jewett had handed out the assignment and Preeti had gone off with her project partner, Chance asked right out, "What was that about? On the bus?"

Martha looked away. "Nothing," she said sharply.

"It wasn't nothing. What's with you and those girls?"

"Nothing's *with* us," Martha said. "They're my friends."

"Maybe they used to be," Chance said, "but not anymore."

Martha was looking at him now, and he had taken a big breath, as if he had all sorts of ideas that he wanted to share with her. "Look," she said, "I have to work with you. But I don't have to listen to you. So will you just stop talking?"

Chance stood perfectly still and looked at her. She waited for him to kick her in the shin or something. She could tell by his tight jaw and the way he wouldn't meet her eyes that he wanted to. "Fine," he said at last. "Tell me the first question."

He got interested in the center pretty soon, especially in Fin, the man who swam down the whole Fraser River, rapids and all—not once, but twice. Martha resisted getting interested herself. Instead, she just trailed after him, collecting the research. Whenever they found themselves near the other girls, she pretended that she didn't care. When it was time for the break, she grabbed her juice and a couple of cookies and slipped away toward the big glass doors. Chance had gone straight for Ken, and they were sitting with that busybody, Doug, so he wasn't going to bother her. Martha tore open her packet of cookies and found herself gazing outside at the wooden promenade. Beyond that was the river. She glanced over her shoulder. Not one person from her group was watching her. She took a bite of cookie and leaned into the door, pushing it open.

It was cold outside, and she wasn't wearing her coat, so she almost turned right around and went back in. It seemed a shame not to step up to the railing, though, and look down at the river. She gripped the cold metal with her free hand, breathing the oily fishy smell and gazing at the water. Shimmery red and blue patches explained the oily part of the smell. To her right, a pier stretched out into the river with a couple of big boats tied up to it. Down a ways, she saw a real paddle wheeler. Beyond the pier, a tugboat strained to tow a log boom upstream.

A scratchy sound pulled her attention back to the pier. She looked to her left and jumped. A crow was sidling along the railing toward her, its beady black eye intent on her remaining cookie.

Martha had never been that close to a crow—or any bird, for that matter. She stared right into its black eye, and the crow stared back, moving its scaly feet every now and again, as if to remind her of the food she held. At last Martha released the railing, tore her eyes off the creature and broke her cookie into pieces.

Turning, she dropped one bit, a quarter maybe, onto the wood near her feet. The crow spread its wings and, somewhat awkwardly, fell upon the scrap of food. Martha watched, delighted, for the seconds it took for the bit of cookie to disappear into the crow. Then she looked up and took a step back.

Several crows and even more seagulls were bearing down upon her.

Unease overtook wonder, and she retreated toward the building, scattering the rest of the cookie as far from her as she could. Well out of the way, she watched the birds battle over the crumbs, screeching and cawing and pecking.

A voice at her shoulder made her jump again.

"Ah. You fed them, didn't you?" Doug said.

She looked up at him. "There was only one crow, and I gave him just a bit," she said. She was mad at Doug, she reminded herself. But then, she had no one else to tell.

The birds were leaving now. They had finished the food and could see that Martha's hands were empty except for a juice box.

"Food brings them out in droves," he said. "Try eating fish and chips at the beach!"

Martha shrugged. She knew better than to eat fish and chips at the beach. Too much sand and dirt, her mother said.

She turned back to watch the crows—who had been scrabbling at her feet a moment ago—flying together over the river.

"They stick together," she said. "The crows."

"Yes," Doug said. "They're pretty bright, those birds." He looked at her. "You know the rules, Martha. Stay with the group. Anyway, the break's over. Chance will be looking for his partner!"

Together, they went back inside. Chance was upon them immediately, looking from one to the other. He settled on Martha.

"Where were you? It's time to get started. We have a lot of questions left to go."

Martha looked down at the paper, but she had to blink twice before she could read the words. She had to clear from her mind the image of that hungry, feathered creature. What went on behind that beady eye? Without thinking, she wrote *crow* and *claw* and *eye* in the margin of the work sheet.

"Hey, you're wrecking it!" said Chance, who had never handed in a tidy work sheet in his life.

In the days following the field trip, Preeti and Sam and Hailey did not speak to Martha again. She tried to tell herself that it didn't matter. Who cared about them anyway? But she knew who cared. She did. She had always been the one they flocked around, and now she was the one they shunned.

She knew that she had brought it on herself, that she had hurt their feelings way back on the day of the nightgown, but she shoved that feeling aside whenever it arose.

They were mean. That was all.

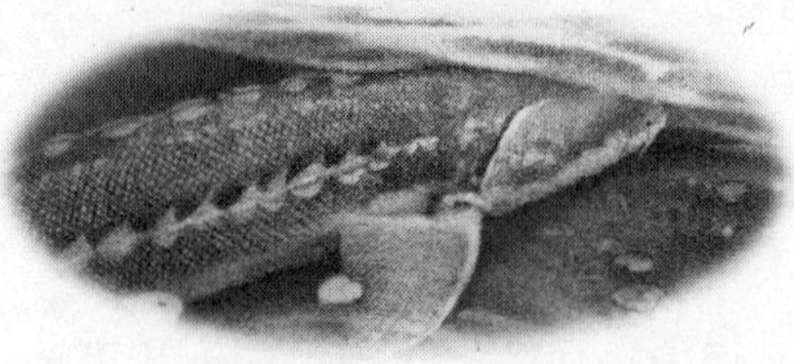

CHAPTER 4

One on One

Two weeks later, Martha looked up from her apple-cinnamon oatmeal. Dad was sitting down at the kitchen table.

"Don't you have to go?" she said.

"Are you so eager to be rid of me?" he replied, smiling.

"No. I...You never sit down in the morning."

"Well, I want to talk to you. "

Martha put down her spoon. The oatmeal felt a bit rumbly in her stomach.

"Where did Mom go?"

"She's upstairs lying down. I'm going to see you off to school this morning."

"But she was right here a minute ago."

Dad's mouth tightened. He took a breath. Martha's breakfast rolled over inside her.

"She needs her rest right now," Dad said. "And today's the day that you see Linda after school, isn't it?"

Martha nodded, not quite meeting his eyes. He knew what day it was. For almost a year now, she had been seeing her birth mother on the last Tuesday of every second month during school. That meant October and December. Why was he asking?

"Well, I just spoke to her, and she has agreed to meet you at school this time. The two of you are going to go out from there."

Now Martha did meet his eyes. "The two of us?"

"I think you're old enough, honey. And Linda's doing really well. You don't need Mom or me along on every outing anymore."

Martha's eyes widened. Dad looked right back at her, calm as calm. Mom was in bed when she should have been helping Martha get ready for school. Mom, who had never let her be alone with her birth mother for one minute in her whole entire life (not even when Martha was being born), was suddenly sending her off on her own and not even coming downstairs to tell her about it. And no one was asking

Martha what she wanted. They obviously didn't care. Neither of them.

They were getting a baby of their own. Martha did not matter anymore.

She wanted to shout, to scream up the stairs at her mother, to confront her father. What if Linda was using drugs again? What if she crashed the car? What if she refused to bring Martha home? But Martha did not scream. She did not shout out her fears.

Instead she held her father's gaze and nodded. "You're right," she said. "I'll be fine on my own." Then she ate every last bit of her oatmeal, grabbed her bag and went to wait for him in the car.

Martha, who never dawdled, was dawdling. Mr. Jewett stood and watched her from his desk. Everyone else was gone.

"Is something wrong, Martha?" he asked.

She flinched. "No. I…I just…" She looked around the room. "I wanted to check on our fish," she said.

"All right," Mr. Jewett said. "Take your time."

The enormous fish was spread out all the way across the floor at the back of the room. Martha had helped Chance a bit with the painting, but he was so messy when he was working that most of the time she just left him to it. And often when he should have been doing math or silent reading, he was back there, banging around, trying to get the paint just the right shade of gray, or fussing over scutes and barbels. Martha could now identify both, thanks to him. Scutes were the rows of sharp white points that ran along the fish's back and sides. Barbels were the four dangly things that hung down in front of the creature's mouth and helped it sense its food. And Mr. Jewett let Chance paint away, just like he let him do everything else. Still, the pointy scutes and the dangly barbels were perfect, Martha thought. She touched the painted surface and tried for a moment to imagine that it was real.

Then she turned to the back wall, where the sturgeon display was. One poster showed the early stages: eggs, larvae, young-of-the-year. She looked at the young-of-the-year for a long time. It was a strange, small, spiky creature.

"Time to go," Mr. Jewett said.

Martha reached out a finger and touched the image. Then she straightened up. Yes, it was time to go.

Martha stood on the school's cement steps and watched Linda suck on a cigarette. When Linda saw Martha, she stubbed the cigarette out with her foot and started across the grass in Martha's direction.

Martha glanced to both sides. Had she stayed inside long enough? The whole area was deserted. Martha breathed in a mixture of relief and misery and darted right past Linda and straight into the backseat of the car, which reeked of stale smoke. Martha had never been inside Linda's car before. She had never been inside any car that smelled of smoke.

Linda was behind her, leaning right in the door. "Hey, you don't have to sit in the backseat, kiddo!"

Linda didn't know one single thing.

"Yes, I do," Martha said stiffly. "Children aren't supposed to sit in the front. It's not safe."

Linda looked puzzled for a moment. "Well, all right then," she said, turning on a great big smile.

"You'd best stay put. I want a hug though. Say hello to your mom!" And she pulled Martha into a stinky embrace.

You're not my mom. You're not my mom.

Martha held herself taut in Linda's bony arms. Linda had never called herself Martha's mom before. She would not do that if Mom were here.

"I'm so excited that we get to spend time together, just the two of us," Linda was saying as she withdrew from the backseat. Her words tumbled over themselves. "Your dad said that we can stay out until nine. If you don't have any homework, that is. Do you?"

Martha opened her mouth to say that she had lots of homework and would certainly need to be home by seven, but Linda wasn't done. "Even if you do have homework, that's okay. We could go to my place right now. You could do it before supper. It would be just like...just like..." She stopped then, but Martha knew what she was thinking, and she did not like it.

"I got all my work done at school," she said, keeping her voice firm. *I will never, ever go to her house,* she thought. The mere idea of it brought fear creeping from where it lurked inside her, right to the center of her belly. She swallowed hard, hunkered down in the backseat and fastened her seatbelt.

She had never felt afraid like this with Linda before, because Mom or Dad had always been there. And Linda always sat up in front with the driver. And Mom or Dad always answered the hard questions. Martha didn't like the hugs, but she had been curious about her birth mother and she had liked telling her about school and stuff. Mom and Dad had helped with that too. Without Mom or Dad there, the woman in the front seat seemed much more real somehow, and much more scary.

They went to Denny's. Martha hated Denny's. She never went there with Mom and Dad. Mom had called it "grungy" the one time Dad suggested it. She had never been there with Linda either, because Mom had always been with them. They had gone to White Spot the first time, last December, and to a Chinese restaurant twice since. Once Mom had suggested Japanese food, but Linda said that she didn't like raw fish.

That was stupid, because you don't have to eat raw fish in a Japanese restaurant. There are lots of other things, like prawn tempura and chicken teriyaki.

Martha flipped through the Denny's menu.

"Hey, it's free for kids under ten today," Linda said. "Here's the kids' menu." She reached across and turned Martha's menu over to the back. Martha was to choose between fish sticks, chicken fingers or a cheeseburger, all with fries. She knew what Mom would say about that. "Do you want to get a milkshake instead of pop?" Linda asked. "I love their milkshakes."

"No, thank you," Martha said.

Linda's smile froze for a moment. Then her eyes crinkled. "Hey," she said, "Halloween comes on a Friday this year!"

"Yeah," Martha said.

"What are you going to be?" Linda asked.

Martha's stomach tightened. She did not want to think about Halloween, and she certainly did not want to talk to Linda about it.

Last year she had been Queen Elizabeth I. Other kids were just ordinary princesses or witches, but she had been a real historical figure, with a heavy wig on her head, white paint on her face and a dress that swept the ground and rose in a big white ruff around her neck. Mom had bought some parts of the costume and made others. At lots of the houses, everyone had come to the door to see, and Dad had come out of the shadows, camera at the ready. Mom had stayed home, in her own scary costume, and handed out candy at the door.

This year, no one had said a word about Halloween. Not one word. On the weekend, Martha had snuck into the storage closet and dug out last year's dress, but she only had to hold it up against herself to see that she had grown too much to wear it again.

Not for a second did she consider telling Linda any of that.

"Dad's taking me shopping tomorrow," she said. "I'm going to pick a brand-new costume."

Linda grinned at her. "That's exciting," she said. "What would you like to be?"

"A princess," Martha said, even though last year she had been a queen. Everyone expected girls to want to be princesses.

They placed their orders then, and silence fell. Linda picked at her paper napkin, reducing part of it to shreds. Martha looked on, disapproving. Her own napkin was on her lap, where it belonged. After a while, Linda smoothed out what was left of her napkin, arranged her knife and fork neatly on top of it and looked up.

There was that grin again, maybe a little shaky at the corners.

"Hey," she said, "you know what?"

Silence.

At last Martha realized what was required of her. "What?" she said.

"I met a guy!"

Martha stared at the skinny, jittery, smoky-smelling woman opposite her. Linda was acting different without Mom there to answer her questions or to tell her things about Martha. Martha wondered for a moment if Linda really was using drugs again. How would Martha even be able to tell?

She collected herself. "That's nice," she said.

"He's so sweet, you know. He's taken me out, what, five times now...and to nice restaurants. He's really interested in me. In *me*, you know. He's in construction."

Martha thought and thought. What could she say to all of this? Then she had an idea. "What's his name?" she said.

Linda beamed. "Brad," she said. "Brad Simmons." She gazed at Martha across the table. "How does Linda Simmons sound to you?"

Martha stared back. Something dark and furious slithered through her. This woman had given Martha away when she was a little tiny baby. And now Martha was supposed to smile and say how pleased she was for her. Well, she wasn't pleased. She wasn't pleased at all.

"We're studying sturgeon at school," she said.

Linda looked confused. A slight qualm made Martha hesitate for a moment. Then another thought occurred to her. "Sturgeon spawn every twelve years."

Linda's brows knit.

"They lay thousands and thousands and thousands of eggs. And then they swim away. Forever," she added. That was the key word.

Forever.

"That's very interesting," Linda said, but her brows stayed knit.

Nervous, Martha thought. She looks nervous.

The food came, and Martha put on her brightest smile. "Oh, the fish sticks look delicious," she said. "Yummy."

It helped to have something to do. Martha ate slowly, smiling over her knife and fork at Linda, who was working away on a burger and fries. Linda smiled back.

"I'm glad that you're learning so much in science," Linda said at one point.

Martha nodded.

"Brad loves fishing," Linda went on. "I think he even caught a sturgeon once. And released it," she added quickly in response to Martha's shocked stare. "You'd like him, you know."

Martha looked down at her plate and took another bite. She would not.

"I thought I'd talk to Denise, and maybe, you know, when we see each other at Christmas, maybe Brad could come too, or maybe you could even come to my place," Linda said, her words tripping over each other.

Martha lowered her head a little farther. Linda was calling Martha's mom Denise. It had been all right when Linda had done that when she was talking directly to Martha's mom. What else was she supposed to call her? But to Martha she had always said "your mom" this and "your mom" that. And every time

Martha had heard "I am not your mom. She is," and she had felt safe. More or less. Now she was alone with Linda, and everything had changed.

How could Mom and Dad make her come out all by herself? All this stuff was their job, not hers. She did not want to meet boyfriends and visit houses. They couldn't make her. Could they?

She grit her teeth and reared her head, bringing her eyes up to Linda's. There: Martha's smile, though small perhaps, was in place. There: her mouth was opening. And words were coming out.

"I don't know," she was saying. "I'd have to ask my mom and dad." She put a little extra emphasis on the word *mom*, but Linda didn't seem to notice.

Her grin widened. "Oh, they'll be fine with it," she said, and Martha's gut twisted.

Linda went right on. "I just know you'll love him," she gushed. "He's so sweet, and he loves kids. You know, he…If we ever got married, I'd be his first wife, you know, his first real partner. And he wants… Well, the wedding first, right? And you would be the sweetest little flower girl!"

Martha's smile stayed in place somehow. She managed to say "Mmhmm" in all the right spots, but after that she counted off the seconds until Linda was steering the car to the curb outside Martha's house. She jumped from the car and had to will her body to stay in place long enough to let Linda hug her goodbye. The hug ended, at last, and Linda got back in her car.

Moments later, Martha shut the front door gently behind her. Dad was on the couch. Mom was nowhere to be seen. Martha stood in the living room entrance.

"Dad," she said, "I don't have a costume for Halloween."

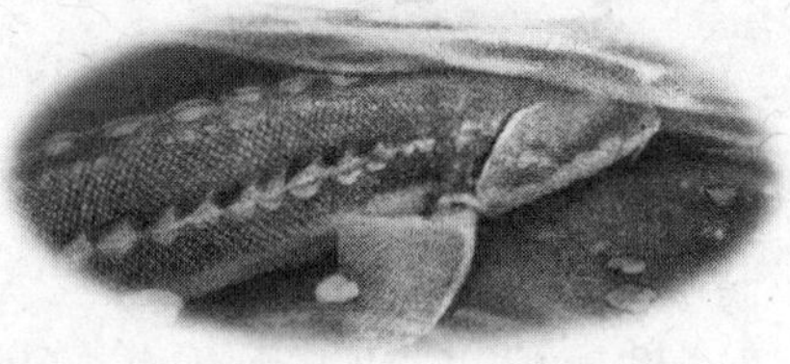

CHAPTER 5

The Scariest Night of the Year

Some of the kids wore their costumes to school on Friday, Chance included. He had obviously made his costume all by himself.

Martha had only just got her costume the night before.

"I'll be taking care of that!" Dad had said brightly when Martha confronted him after her awful dinner.

"How?" Martha had shot back. "Halloween's in three days."

"That's lots of time for a shopping expedition," he said, beaming at her and whipping his wallet out of his back pocket.

Martha did not beam. She did not like the idea of shopping for a costume so close to Halloween, or with her father, who did not care about things the same way her mother did. And she was worried about Halloween itself. Last year, she and Preeti had talked about trick-or-treating together this year. They were going to be in grade four; Halloween should no longer be only a family affair. "Maybe your dad could take us," Preeti had said.

Last year, when Martha had worn her Queen Elizabeth I costume to school, everyone had *oohed* and *aahed* over it in a highly satisfactory way. Martha had glowed with pride. Now Preeti was not speaking to her, and Martha knew that any costume her father bought her two days before the big day was not likely to impress.

It turned out that there would be no shopping two days before. Dad had a meeting after work on Wednesday. The shopping took place on Thursday, the day before Halloween, and Dad took her to a department store, not a costume shop. The racks were almost bare. Martha considered going without a costume and hiding away in her room all evening, but her dad was smiling as he pawed through the racks, showing her a ratty witch's cape and hat and, of all things, a ghost costume. He held up a few old Disney things too, but all the ones from recent movies were gone, probably long gone…

Then she saw, behind the rack, in a heap on the floor, what looked like a fish's tail. She reached down and picked it up. A mermaid. Ariel. She gazed at it, trying to imagine.

"Dad," she said, "I think that I would like to be a fish."

"A fish," he said.

"Yes," she replied. "Here's the tail. I could wear a gray shirt and we could make some fins and scutes."

"Scutes?" he said.

"Yeah," she said, impatient with him. "Now, all I need is a mask. A fish mask."

Dad let fall the gauzy princess skirt he was holding. "A fish mask?"

Was he going to repeat *everything* she said?

"We can go to a real costume store, Dad. It's only four thirty. I'll bet they're open late today."

Dad took a step away from the costume rack. "Sweetie," he said, but the word was crisp around the edges, "we're not going to go to a 'real costume store.' We're not going to go to *any* other store. I left work early to help you with this. It's suppertime, and I, for one, am starving. You need to pick a costume here. Now."

Martha stared at her father. Last year, Mom would have found a way to buy her a fish mask, or make her one, no matter how close to Halloween it was. Now Mom was lying down at home, and Dad was bossing her around. She felt her whole face contract. Then she thought of her mother at the sewing machine trying to find a way to make her daughter look like a fish. Martha had been an English queen, a Japanese princess, a Bollywood dancer. But turn her into a fish? Mom liked to make Martha look pretty, not like some creature of the deeps. It would never happen. She almost smiled. She looked at her father again. He was positively scowling. She squared her shoulders.

"I want to be a fish. I don't see why we can't go to another store." She paused. Then she lied. "Mom would take me," she said.

Half an hour later, she was running from the garage into the house, letting the door slam behind her. Who cared if Mom was resting and it woke her up?

She dashed through the kitchen, up the stairs and into her room, where she slammed another door.

Ariel. Dad had bought the Ariel costume. He had positively refused to take her anywhere else. He had told her not to act so spoiled, to think about somebody else for a change. He had even taken hold of her upper arm, hard, when she shouted back at him. She bet there were marks.

She threw herself down on her bed. How had everything changed so fast?

Dad's meanness turned out to be a blessing when Chance turned up at school on Friday morning decked out as a really weird sturgeon. He had no fish mask, but he wore a gray ski mask, gray pants and a gray sweatshirt. He had used a whole lot of duct tape to stick rows of scutes made from white Bristol board down his back and sides. And four barbels made from thin rubber tubing dangled from the wool above his upper lip. Martha peered at them from a distance. Dozens of staples held them there. He had taped fins on in all the right places, but they flopped about oddly as he walked. The one blessing was that he had not tried to make one of those gross hose-like mouths that sturgeon had.

Martha shuddered. Didn't Chance have a mirror in his house? How could Doug and Angie let him out like that?

Imagine if she had turned up dressed like a sturgeon too! It was bad enough that her costume had a fish's tail. She was glad that she had come to school costumeless, leaving Ariel in a heap on her bedroom floor, even though the sprightly mermaid would have fit right in with Preeti's and Sam's and Hailey's costumes, all straight off the rack.

By the time Halloween night was over, Martha already wished that she could forget her whole grade-four trick-or-treating experience.

To begin with, she had the most pathetic costume of her life.

Then, as they were eating an astonishing dinner of boiled hot dogs and carrot sticks, Mom put her hand over her mouth and stood.

“Excuse me,” she said and rushed to the bathroom.

Martha could hear her throwing up all the way from the table. Dad almost knocked over his chair in his hurry to be at her side.

Mom had thrown up lots in the summer, but it had almost stopped by the time school started. Something was not right.

The doorbell rang. Martha could hear the giggles from the front step. The first trick-or-treaters were outside. She looked at the bathroom door, firmly closed.

“Can you answer it?” Dad shouted.

Martha ran to the front door and opened it. A small robot looked up at her. “Waaall-ee,” it said and held out a big sack. Martha almost smiled. She turned to the hall table, where the bowl of candy should have been. Nothing.

“Hold on a minute,” she said to the friendly little robot. She knew that the candy was in the house. They had bought bags and bags last night, along with the mermaid costume. Seconds later, she was back at the door, ripping open a bag of mini chocolate bars and shoving three of them into the gaping sack.

“Thank you,” Wall-E said.

When Martha turned away from the door, there were Mom and Dad, side by side. Mom looked gray. Dad looked worried.

"I can't leave your mother to take you out, honey," he said. "Dr. Storey said to keep an eye—"

Mom managed a small smile as she interrupted. "Dr. Storey's a worrywart," she said, "and Peter, so are you." She turned to Martha. "But do you think you could you call a friend?" Her voice was strained, as if vomit might leak out with the words.

"How about Preeti?" Dad said.

Martha tried not to let panic show on her face. "Preeti's busy," she said abruptly. She couldn't call Preeti. She just couldn't.

"Peter," Mom said, her voice a bit stronger. "Give Doug and Angie a call."

It took Martha a moment, even once she heard the names, to understand what her mother was up to. And when she did get it, she couldn't believe it. Her mother was trying to send her out into the street, into public, with the weirdest boy in class. And, just to top it off, that weird boy would be dressed in old clothes, duct tape, Bristol board and staples…with rubber tubes hanging off his face.

She opened her mouth to express her resistance. She sent messages to her legs to carry her up the stairs to her room—she would slam the door and never ever come out. But her mouth stayed shut, and her legs stayed still as she tried to take in what was going on.

Her mother was throwing up all of a sudden. And Mom and Dad had been keeping a secret: the doctor had told them to watch for something. That was why Dad had almost knocked his chair over following Mom to the bathroom. They hadn't even bothered to tell their own daughter that there was something to worry about. Self-pity washed through her, right down to her toes, self-pity mixed with a little bit of fear.

At last her legs released her, and she headed off to dress herself up as a silly little mermaid. She took the stairs one at a time and turned her eyes away from the loving family of three that smiled down from photo after photo after photo up the stairwell. Behind her, Dad picked up the phone. She heard his end of the conversation—short, friendly. He said goodbye before she was even halfway to her room.

"Doug and Chance will be by in a few minutes," Dad said to her back, not even seeming to care that she didn't turn around.

Dad was at the door handing out candy to two fairies and a Shrek when she came back down. Doug and Chance the Homemade Sturgeon were already there, right outside on the sidewalk. Martha passed her father without a glance and joined the enemy. What else could she do?

Worry about her mother had found a spot inside her, and she left it there, all tucked away. It was hard to think about all that stuff anyway in the face of Chance's chatter, which brought on annoyance, and in the face of the Halloween atmosphere that filled the streets, which brought on a kind of begrudging joy.

So when Martha was brought up short by the sound of her own name, she was actually gasping with pleasure at the sight of a front yard done up exactly like a cemetery.

"Look, it's Martha...and Chance. A girl with a fish tail and...a fish!"

It was Sam who had spoken. Preeti, Sam and Hailey had stopped mid-cemetery, and Hailey's face was wide-open in laughter. Preeti was behind the other two, frozen in mid-step.

Pleasure departed. Shame took its place.

"Hi, girls," Doug said. "Would you like to join us?"

"No," Martha said before Sam could speak another word. "No, it's okay." And she fixed her eyes on the cement walkway, shoved past Chance and barreled right between the other girls, casting them to both sides as she made for the front door of the cemetery house. "Trick or treat!" she shouted as she knocked.

At least it was Friday. Maybe by Monday, they would have forgotten.

An angry tear spurted onto her right cheek. I'm supposed to be out with them, she thought. I'm supposed to be one of the popular ones.

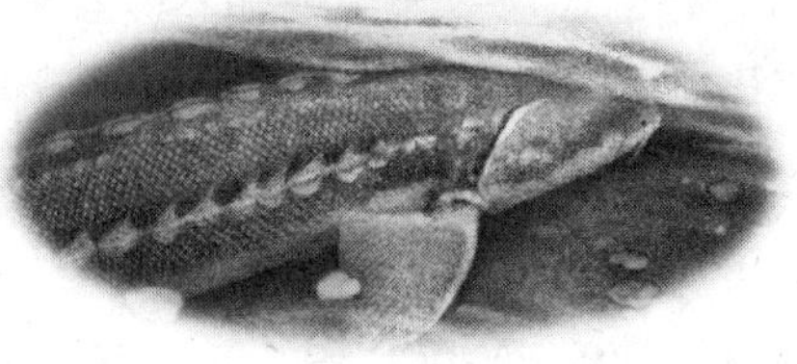

CHAPTER 6

A Girl?

The next Monday afternoon, Mom was not lying on the couch when Martha got home from school. She was at the kitchen table, staring at something. She looked up when Martha came in. Her face was shining as if she had a great big lightbulb stuffed inside her head.

Martha tried to smile back.

"Oh, sweetheart, come here." Her mother was holding out her hands. Martha had no choice but to walk over and submit her own hands to her mother's.

"Your dad and I went to the doctor today," she said. She waited as if she thought Martha might say something. At last she went on. "For the ultrasound."

Martha knew what that was. Mom and Dad had told her. They had even offered to take her along, but she had said that she shouldn't miss school.

An ultrasound was when the doctor rubbed something like a camera on the mother's stomach so you could see the baby inside her. You could tell if there was something wrong, and sometimes you could see if it was a boy or a girl.

Mom held out the thing she had been looking at. It was a weird, swirly black-and-white picture. "Look," Mom said. "There she is."

Martha just stared. She could see the baby now, or fetus, or whatever it was. It didn't look like a person exactly, but she could see its head and its body. A girl. That was what Mom was saying. Mom was going to have a girl baby.

At last, Martha managed to pull her eyes away from the picture and up to her mother's shining face. "That's nice," she said.

Mom looked at her. "There's something else," she said.

Martha looked back. Her mother's face was not all joy now. "The baby's doing well," she said slowly, "and so am I..."

Something was wrong. Something was definitely wrong. The fear that had stayed tucked away over the weekend slithered out and made a mad dash into Martha's belly.

"You know how I got sick on Friday, and your dad stayed home with me? I said he was a worry-wart." She smiled. "And he is. You know it. And I know it."

Come on, Martha thought. Tell me what's wrong.

"Well, the doctor says that Peter is right to worry a little bit. I need to take it easy. She's not putting me on bed rest, but I need to slow down, keep my feet up as much as I can. There are still almost three more months to go before the baby's due. Dr. Storey doesn't want her to come early. And neither do I."

Martha opened her mouth to say something, but she didn't know what to say. The fear had slithered back into its hiding place while Mom talked. Rest didn't sound so bad. She had already been resting half the time anyway. "Okay, Mom," Martha said finally. "I have to go to my room. I have lots of homework."

She saw Mom's face fall, but it was the best she could do. It really was.

On Thursday, Mom wasn't on the couch, and she wasn't at the kitchen table. Surely she wouldn't be out when Martha got home. Martha had seen the car in the garage.

Instead of shouting, she climbed the stairs, one at a time, stopping to look at each photo on the wall as she went. Mom had put them up just last year, so they showed almost the whole of Martha's life and one picture from before. That one, the one at the very top of the stairs, was Martha's favorite. It was Mom and Dad's wedding photo, from years before Martha came along, and she knew every detail by heart. The photograph was black and white, taken on a beach. Dad looked like a movie star in his fancy suit—a tuxedo. And Mom looked more beautiful than anyone Martha had ever seen. She was barefoot, holding her long white skirt up off the sand, so that her legs showed. She had pearls around her neck, and her hair was kind of blown around. She was looking into the camera and laughing. Dad was looking at her.

Martha stopped and gazed at it for a long time before she took the last step to the upstairs and went to see if her mom was in bed. She wasn't. Martha shut the bedroom door and stood still for a moment. The house was silent. She felt a hint of panic.

But no. There were still more places to look.

Mom was not in Martha's bedroom. She wasn't in the spare room. That left one more place. The door to the baby-to-be's room was ajar. Martha put her hand on the white wooden surface and pushed. There was Mom, sitting in the new rocking chair, fast asleep. Martha stepped inside the baby-to-be's room for the first time since Mom and Dad had dragged her in there right after announcing the pregnancy.

"Come help us decide what to do with the room," Dad had said.

Martha had wanted to say, *No, that's okay. You decide*. But she hated to hurt their feelings. She had gone, and she had nodded at their ideas and looked thoughtful when they asked her questions. But she had been glad that she happened to be at summer camp when they were getting the room all cleared up. And she had managed to miss out on both shopping trips so far.

Now it looked as if Mom had been on another one. Of course she had. Now she knew the baby was a girl!

Paint chips and bits of fabric were scattered on the new change table, and Mom had draped a fuzzy pink baby blanket over her chest. She had a piece of paper in her hand. Martha moved farther into the room.

It was the swirly baby picture. The new daughter: her *sister*. Martha tried out the word, but it just didn't fit. Before Mom could wake up and catch her there, Martha left the room and went down to the kitchen to get a snack. All by herself.

After supper the following Wednesday, Dad motioned Martha to join him on the couch. Mom was upstairs lying down.

"She needs lots of rest," Dad said. "The doctor says it's best for the baby and it's best for her."

"I know," Martha said. "Mom told me." She tilted her head slightly and let her brows pull together just a bit: that was her listening face.

"Your mom is forty-four years old," Dad said.

Martha nodded. She knew that too.

"That's older than most women who have babies," he went on, "so she has to be a little bit more careful. She has to rest a lot."

Martha nodded again, even though she was sure there was more to it than that. Preeti's mother had a baby last year, and she had to be just as old as Mom. She had gray hair! And even when her stomach stuck out way farther than Mom's, she had gone to work and picked Preeti up from school and done all sorts of things.

"This means that we are going to need your help, Martha," Dad said.

This time Martha didn't nod. Her tongue came loose from her teeth.

"I do help," she said, her voice rising. "I get my own breakfast every day now. I make my bed. I get my own snacks." She paused to draw breath. "I help and I help and I help."

Dad's breath made a little whooshing noise. "Well," he said, "I think that you could to do a bit more than that. I think that it's time you started making your own school lunches. And tonight you could help Mom unload the dishwasher."

Martha opened her mouth to ask why he couldn't help Mom or just unload the dishwasher himself, but something in his face stopped her. He looked determined, but more than that. He almost looked a little bit scared.

"Okay, Dad," she said.

CHAPTER 7

Stupid Fish

The drive went on and on and on, but Martha was too wrapped up in her thoughts to take it in. On Wednesday, Dad had instructed her to make her own lunches and unload the dishwasher. On Friday, he had told her that she was spending the next day with Angie and Doug.

He was shipping her out.

Now, in the car, Chance talked excitedly and endlessly to his foster parents. Well, at the beginning he tried to talk to Martha, but she showed him her still, silent face. He stared at her for a long moment, shrugged and directed his next words to the front seat.

How old were the sturgeon they were going to see? Why did sturgeon live at a salmon hatchery?

What went on at a hatchery anyway? Was this a good time to go? November?

Doug and Angie took turns answering as best they could. Chance knew a lot of the answers already. Angie had a bundle of papers on her lap, printed from a government website. She had spent the first hour in the car reading all that stuff out loud.

"Who cares?" Martha had wanted to scream at them then. And "Who cares?" she wanted to scream at them now.

Stupid fish.

She fixed her gaze on the Fraser River, the occasional tugboat, the endless logging operations, the flat land on the other side and the hills in the distance. Then they left the river and drove beside a railroad track that ran on raised ground higher up than the car. She wished she would see a train. She wished she were *on* a train.

Without warning, the car stopped, just stopped, right in the middle of the road.

"Look up," Doug said.

Martha looked. And gasped. The trees ahead of them were huge, craggy, leafless. And full of eagles. She pushed the button and the window slid down.

Cool air and the scent of pine trees washed over her as she craned her neck outside. Eagles. The closest one was so big that she couldn't even take all of it in. She could see its sharp beak and its eyes. She could swear that it was staring right at her. She stared back.

It gave its head a small toss, spread an enormous pair of wings and lifted off. She heard the scratching sound as its claws left the branch and the *whoosh* of its wings against the air. It flew right over the car, and she couldn't see it anymore. Slowly, she came back to herself. Her head was tipped right back on her neck. Her mouth was wide-open. She twitched, pulled herself together and drew her head back inside the car.

Chance was staring right at her. Martha looked back at him for a moment. He didn't say anything. Well. Let him stare. What did it matter to her? She swung her head back to look out the window again and waited for Doug to drive on.

The hatchery was only about two minutes ahead. They drove through a narrow entrance into a large irregular paved area with a building on their left and a bunch of long cement tanks in front. Doug parked, and Chance had the door open instantly. He practically danced out of the car.

Martha didn't even put a hand on the door handle. They could make her come, but they could not make her get out of the car. She was staying right where she was.

Angie swung her legs out onto the pavement. Chance was already almost at the tanks. "Chance," Angie called, "let's read the sign first." Doug had started toward a big wooden sign, and Angie was right behind him.

Martha snorted. Read a sign! They thought that Chance should read a sign? *That* was a joke. This whole trip was a joke. She tucked her feet tight under the seat in front of her and stared at her knees.

"Hey, you guys! Come on!"

Chance was over by the nearest tank, shouting and waving his arms. "You guys! You've got to see this!" And as he said the last words, something flashed behind him, something he had not seen, but Martha had. She stared past him at the tank and willed it to happen again.

A fish. A fish jumped up out of the tank and into view, right into the air. Chance saw that one and began leaping about in addition to all the shouting and arm-waving. With as much dignity as she could muster, Martha opened the car door and got out. Angie and Doug were rushing to Chance's side. Martha was not about to run. But whatever was in that tank, she might as well see it. She might as well.

Still, she couldn't help herself, she pulled back a bit when she looked in, and her face opened up into surprise and excitement. The tank was full of fish: great big fish with weird pointy noses. They were trying to swim, all in the same direction, but the tank ended and they could go no farther. Every little while, in an extra effort, a burst of strength and determination, a fish leaped into the air.

"Chum," Chance said. "They're chum salmon. They're here to spawn." He looked at Martha. "You know. Lay eggs and fertilize them."

Martha glared at him. What did he think she was, a moron?

They could have pulled out her fingernails, and she would not have admitted it, but she loved everything about the hatchery. Everything, that is, except for the bouncy boy who never allowed a moment's silence. So she lagged behind. She let Chance and

Doug and Angie discover everything together. And she discovered the same things afterward, alone: the spot where the fish had to slither or jump up a level to get into the tank; the spot where tank turned to stream; the realization that the fish were swimming upstream, against the current. Other tanks, higher up and covered with netting, held tiny fish. Fry, Martha thought, surprised at herself for remembering and filled with joy at the sight of all those tiny, tiny creatures. She turned to continue on her way and stopped to look at the narrow, swift-moving stream running under a pretty wooden bridge.

She walked forward, stood on the bridge and gazed down into the tumbling water. Something shot forward. A fish had just swum under the bridge. Martha turned quickly and saw it swim on upstream, another fish close beside. She turned back and stared into the water some more. The bottom of the stream was covered in round orange spheres.

Eggs.

The salmon were spawning! They really were!

Not far beyond the bridge, a pier was built out into a big pond surrounded by trees. Doug and Angie and Chance were leaning over a railing pointing at something in the water. Angie had her camera in her hands. That must be the sturgeon pond.

Martha watched the stream some more, waiting for the others to move on. They did not. At last, she left the bridge and wandered in their direction. Doug looked up and beckoned, his smile enormous. Martha hung back.

The others stayed where they were, held by whatever they saw in that water. Eventually, she stepped off the dirt path onto the wooden pier. Chance looked up. "Hey!" he said. "You've got to see this."

Every bit of Martha rebelled at seeing anything that Chance had seen first. At least, every bit but the soles of her feet, because they kept lifting off and setting down and carrying her closer and closer. "Come on," he whispered as she approached, "she's just here now." Martha took the last three steps a little faster and grasped the railing, leaning out over the water and looking down into the stillness past her reflection and Chancc's beside her. Then she saw it. Gliding through the water, smooth and sleek and enormous, was a sturgeon. It was gray—gray and calm and beautiful. She leaned out a little farther.

"Isn't it amazing?" Chance said.

Martha nodded dreamily. She agreed.

That night, back in her bedroom, she lay awake for a long time, pondering. Birds and fish, fish and birds. Her brain teemed with living things.

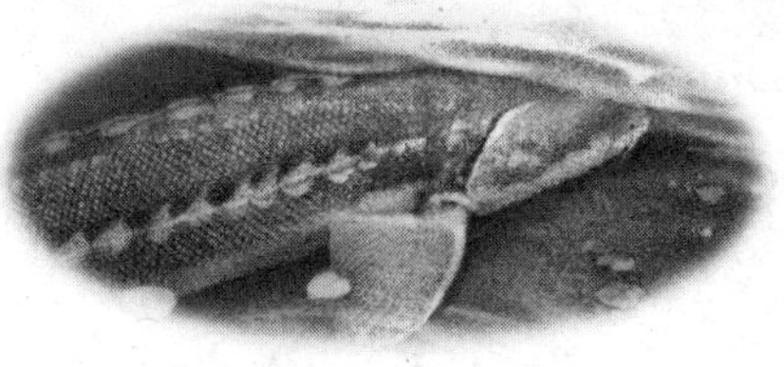

CHAPTER 8

Real Mom

The following weeks passed in a blur of schoolwork (most of it somehow sturgeon-related) and helping out at home while Mom rested. Martha learned to load and unload the dishwasher all by herself. She made her own lunches. She picked out her own clothes.

She still had to pass inspection, though, before she left the house. Each morning, Martha matched: green tights with a green striped shirt; a purple skirt with a white top with purple embroidery around the neck and sleeves, and a purple headband. She felt a rush of comforting warmth when her mother smiled and reached a hand out to stroke her arm.

"You look lovely, Martha," Mom would say. "Do you have a piece of fruit in your lunch?"

Martha would smile back. "An apple," she would reply, or "a cut-up orange. And carrots too."

Those were the best moments of the day.

December arrived. The baby was due in less than two months now. And fish were eclipsed by all the celebrations of the season: Christmas, Hanukkah, Kwanzaa, winter solstice, Ramadan. Usually Martha loved every bit of it, all the music and color at school, along with the building excitement at home.

This year, though, the excitement at home was missing.

Martha and Dad finally put up the tree in the middle of the month, two weeks later than usual. And they did it on their own, with Mom watching from the couch, so it did not look as good as it usually did, even though everything matched—the red lights, the red and gold ornaments. The tree came from a catalogue and was supposed to be one of the best artificial trees you could buy. It was almost brand-new, but when Martha and Dad were done, it looked a little odd, just a bit crooked, perhaps.

"Thank you for doing that," Mom said when they were done and Dad had made them all hot chocolate. "I can't imagine Christmas without a tree!"

Martha was pretty sure that—doctor's instructions or no doctor's instructions—Mom had been aching to get up there and do it properly.

As for the usual gifts with their expensive wrapping paper and pretty ribbons, there were none under the tree yet. But surely they would show up before Christmas did. Surely they would. Mom wasn't up to much shopping though, and Dad was a terrible shopper, so Martha kept reminding herself not to expect much.

Linda was supposed to pick Martha up the day before Christmas Eve, and she was late, as usual. Martha was up in her room when the doorbell rang. She wouldn't go. She just wouldn't. But she knew she had to.

She looked at herself in the mirror.

Tonight, she had decided, she was going to dress to please herself, not her mother. She felt a little worried about what Mom would say, but it was exciting to root through her drawers and closet trying different combinations. What she came up with had flair. It really did! She was wearing navy tights, a black corduroy skirt with a beaded panel down one side, a plain deep blue long-sleeved shirt and a purple velvet tank top. As a final touch, she twisted a thick strand of her hair and used a sparkly clip to hold it in place. Her favorite boots would complete the ensemble.

"Congratulations!" Mom was saying to Linda downstairs when Martha came out of her room.

Martha paused, still out of sight at the top of the stairs.

"We're not going to make a big deal of it," Linda said.

Of what?

"We're thinking we might just go off to Hawaii."

"Mmm. That would be nice," Mom said. "Peter and I got married on the beach in Maui. Barefoot!"

Married? Already?

"Martha!" Mom called. "Linda is here."

Martha backed up a step. "I'm coming!" she shouted, louder than need be.

In the car, they had barely pulled away from the curb before Linda turned all the way around in her seat. While she was driving. "Brad and I are getting married," she said, her face alight.

Martha forced a smile and pointed to an oncoming car. Linda turned her eyes back to the road. Now that Martha thought about it, Linda had seemed a lot happier when they had seen each other in October. Martha had thought it was because her mom wasn't with them. Now she realized that it had probably been because of Brad. She sniffed cautiously. The smell of smoke in the car was almost gone. Had Linda quit smoking?

"That's nice," Martha said, far too long after Linda's announcement. "When?"

"Soon, I think," Linda said. "It depends on Brad. On when he can get away for a bit."

"Oh," Martha said.

The conversation stalled. Linda drove in silence and pulled into the parking lot of their trusty Denny's.

Seats were found. Food was ordered. Food was received.

"I can't miss school," Martha said.

"Miss school?" Linda echoed.

"You know. For Hawaii. The flower girl. I might not be able to..."

Linda had been staring at her, but now she looked down at her plate.

"Oh, honey, it's going to be the tiniest little wedding. Only Brad's parents and his brother, really." She met Martha's eyes. "And you're quite right not to want to miss school. There's nothing more important than education!"

The last words were hard and shiny, like a string of plastic beads popping out of Linda's mouth all in a rush. And Martha understood. They had never intended to take her with them to Hawaii. Never.

I didn't want to go anyway, she reminded herself as she took another bite. She stopped mid-chew. Linda was staring at something over Martha's shoulder, and that something had spread a great big mushy smile all over her face.

"Brad!" she said, but Martha had already guessed.

He had snuck up on them somehow: a big, dark-haired, bearded man in a brown leather jacket who bent down and kissed Linda full on the mouth before turning toward Martha, his face one huge toothy grin. Brad.

"You must be Martha," he said, reaching for her with two great paws.

He wants to hug me, Martha thought, and she glued her back firmly to the back of the bench, arms tight at her sides. Brad drew away, just a bit.

"Brad, this is my daughter, Martha!" Linda said. "And Martha, this is my fiancé, Brad!"

"It's nice to meet you, Brad," Martha said, her voice quiet.

"You too, young lady! You too."

Young lady? Yuck!

Brad had his hand on Linda's shoulder, but he didn't sit down. "It took me almost an hour to get here. Traffic. I'll be back in a minute." And he took off toward the washrooms.

"So, what do you think?" Linda said as soon as he was out of sight.

"Think?" Martha echoed. She dragged her eyes from Linda's stomach, which she'd noticed was a bit poochy under her T-shirt—what if Linda was pregnant too?—up to her glowing face.

"Of Brad, honey!" Linda said, brows raised and lips stretched into an eager smile.

She was so eager, Martha was almost embarrassed for her.

"He's…"

She paused and heard Linda take a breath.

"He's nice."

Linda's eyes widened. "Yeah, he really is! He's going to be a good husband. And maybe, one day, a good father too!"

Martha tensed. She already had a father. Then she looked at Linda's stomach again. Linda was not referring to her. She was referring to a new baby, Linda and Brad's baby.

Martha's own birth father swam, uninvited, into her mind. She did not think about him often. Linda had never told her who her he was. Sometimes she thought that Linda didn't even know. Martha had heard of that. Or maybe he was dead.

Dead.

Martha concentrated on that word. It was so flat and strong and even.

And there was Brad, back at the table, very much alive, but *not* her father, kissing Linda once again, firmly, on the mouth, which was just gross, grinning way too much and sliding himself onto the bench beside Linda.

"Did you tell her about Kelowna?" he said right away, before he even picked up a menu.

"Kelowna?" Martha echoed. "I thought you were getting married in Maui."

Linda put a hand on Brad's arm, but he had already started talking. "Yes, we're *getting married* in Maui, but we're *moving* to Kelowna. I grew up there. Great town!"

Martha sank a little deeper onto the bright orange Denny's bench.

His words were even harder than Linda's. They fell out of his mouth onto the table like great big stones.

"Moving?"

"That's right. Surrey just isn't the best place for Linda. She needs a fresh start. And my mother loves her. Just loves her."

What did he mean? Why did Linda need a fresh start?

"There's lots of construction work there for me," he said. "And we can live with the parents for a while. Mom can use Linda's help. And then maybe we'll rent a little house."

Martha felt sick. Kelowna would mean overnight visits. She had never once spent the night with Linda.

"So I won't be able to see you as often," Linda said softly.

Martha felt herself spiraling downward, a whooshing feeling in the back of her head. She waited for the parachute to open, but it did not. Linda's eyes were not hungry anymore. Her chest had filled out a bit since October. New husbands. New homes. New babies. Her mothers were abandoning her.

Martha was shocked to find herself smiling and nodding.

She ordered a sundae.

"You're just picking at your dessert," Linda said a bit later, around a mouthful of brownie.

Martha shoved her feelings aside once again and took a small bite.

Brad lifted a forkful of blueberry pie and laughed. "Our kid, when we have one…he's going to be a big eater!"

Martha took another tiny bite, but it seemed reluctant to go down her throat. By the time the bill came, her ice cream and butterscotch sauce was a big melted mess.

They left Linda's car behind in the parking lot. "We'll pick it up on the way back to my place," Brad said.

Martha shuddered. She didn't want to think about anybody going to anybody's place.

In the backseat of Brad's car, she wondered what it would be like if they kidnapped her. What if the car continued on past her house, onto the freeway toward Hope? She was pretty sure that was the way to Kelowna.

She would jump out at the first stoplight, she decided. Then she caught her breath. What if the car had those kid-locks? She'd be trapped. She thought some more.

A cell phone. Brad must have a cell phone. She'd steal it and call home.

Martha looked out the car window. She had to keep track of her location so she could describe it. The location was familiar. Brad slowed down and turned left, and Martha realized they'd just come from a different direction than she was used to. There was her house, same as always. The car pulled to a stop, and Linda swiveled in her seat and reached a hand back in Martha's direction.

No kidnapping then.

Martha's eyes stung. She wanted to slug that man in the back of the head. How dared they so cheerfully get married and move away? And who cared anyway? She hoped she never saw either of them again. Never!

"Your Christmas present is in that little bag on the seat next to you," Linda said. "I think we might be moving before you and I are supposed to meet in February. I'll call Denise and tell her all our plans. We'll sort things out."

My mom, Martha thought. You'll call *my mom*. Not *Denise*! Martha wished she was brave enough to say the words out loud.

She opened the door and slid out of the car, the Christmas bag dangling from one hand. Her body felt like cement.

"So long, kid," Brad said, looking over his shoulder.

Linda was beside the car too. She held out her arms. "Come here, honey," she said. "Come here and give me a hug."

Martha dragged her heavy body and her stinging eyes around the car door and into Linda's arms. Linda smelled faintly of sweat and some flowery perfume. Martha ordered her own arms to hug back. And then it was done.

"Merry Christmas, sweetheart."

Sweetheart?

"I'll call Denise soon."

"Yeah, okay," Martha said, the muscles in her back stiffening further. *She's my mom. My mom. My mom!* She watched Linda swing her legs back into the car, close the door and open the window.

"Goodbye," Brad called as the car pulled away.

"Goodbye, honey." That was Linda, of course.

"Goodbye," Martha said, but she was pretty sure her voice was too quiet for them to hear.

Linda trailed her arm out the window in a small wave, and then they were gone.

Martha looked at the house. The door was closed. No one had heard the car pull up, or, if they had, they had not come out. *I am alone*, Martha thought. Then, "I am alone," she said out loud. "I am alone."

Then she tried out another line: "I am alone. And lonely."

Back straight, cement softened slightly, she marched up thc walk toward her own front door.

CHAPTER 9

Alone

The Christmas season was not unfolding as usual. Martha did not need to be told that Christmas would not be normal. She could see it. The mess in the house got worse and worse. Meals got simpler and simpler.

No one went shopping or took Martha shopping. Martha had some money—weeks of allowances collected in her green-and-pink-beaded wallet. She even had some ideas. But she had no opportunities. Also, she knew that she needed to buy an extra gift this year. She needed to buy a gift for the new baby. And she didn't want to.

“This is going to be her first Christmas,” Mom had said one morning, weeks ago.

Dad had looked up and grinned.

“But the baby’s not coming till the end of January,” Martha had protested.

Mom smiled and looked down. She put a hand on her stomach. “The baby might not be coming *out* till January, but she’s here right this minute. She’s been kicking and wiggling for months!”

I know! I know! I know! Martha wanted to shout. *I felt her move, didn’t I? I did what you wanted. Now, shut up!*

She squeezed her lips together and stared at her plate.

“Anyway,” Mom said, “let’s include her in Christmas. Let’s give her little gifts. And you can film it, Peter. We’ll have it to show her later.”

Dad had grinned some more, his hand plastered over Mom’s hand on that baby belly. Martha had finished her microwaved meal and escaped to the TV.

She had been feeling sad about Christmas ever since, but she couldn't help but feel a little bit hopeful too. After all, it was Christmas! And even if they were going to give that baby presents, the baby still wouldn't be there, not really. It was still Martha's last Christmas as an only child.

But how could she get up on Christmas morning and enjoy herself if she had nothing to give? Mom and Dad probably hadn't got her much. But she would get her stocking for sure and at least one or two presents. There had to be one or two!

Martha had tossed and turned a bit lately thinking about presents. When she got home from her night out with Linda and Brad, she almost decided that she didn't care. Mom was in bed asleep when Martha got inside, and she didn't even wake up to say goodnight. Dad was dozing in front of the TV. Martha wandered into the living room, dropped the bag with Linda's gift and stood looking down at her father.

Almost immediately his eyes blinked open.

"How was your evening?" he said in his sleepy voice.

"I met Linda's boyfriend, Brad," Martha said.

"Brad, eh?" Dad said. His voice didn't sound sleepy anymore. "Did you like him?"

That's not the point, Martha screamed inside her head. But all she said was, "He was okay, I guess. They might be moving to Kelowna." She watched his face, and he met her eyes.

"Kelowna? That's a ways away."

"Yes," Martha said.

He sat up. "Well, I'm sure Linda will make the trip to the big city regularly, Martha," he said. "Anyway, you haven't seemed that keen on the visits recently."

Keen on the visits? Her birth mother didn't even care about her enough to stay in the same city, and that was all Dad could say?

"Goodnight, Dad," Martha said.

He reached up, pulled her toward him and kissed the top of her head.

I used to love that, Martha thought, as she resisted the urge to stamp on his foot. "Night," she said and darted away from him up the stairs.

She tossed and turned for a long time that night. Mom and Dad were clueless. Clueless! And they didn't even care. All they cared about was that new baby.

And she didn't have presents for them. And Christmas was going to be awful!

She must have slept in the end, because she woke up and it was morning. It was Christmas Eve morning. And she had an idea.

The cardboard box was in the back of her closet. She pulled on her thick winter robe, slid her feet into fleecy slippers, turned the light on in her closet and crawled in right to the back, where the roof sloped down. She had to move a couple of other boxes to get at the one she wanted, and it was a bit dusty in there, but she managed. She lifted the lid off the box and settled down cross-legged to dig. The box contained books that she had supposedly outgrown. Some of them had belonged to Mom or Dad when they were little, but they had written *For Martha* in the front of the books, so they were hers now. One or two had even belonged to Mom's mom. *When We Were Very Young, Goodnight Moon, Possum Magic, Something From Nothing, Max and Ruby.* All those books came out of the box. She had to keep digging to find the last one. There it was, right in the bottom: *Where the Wild Things Are.*

Martha tucked the lid of the box closed, gathered her selections together and made her way out of the closet. She sat with the books and a pen for a long time, uncertain, but at last she knew what words to inscribe, and she wrote them, feeling a surge of pleasure at the sight of her beautiful handwriting adorning a beloved book. Then she went downstairs and got wrapping paper from last Christmas, a big floppy ribbon, scissors and tape. Back in her room, she did her best to make a pretty package. It went out of sight under the bed, and she headed downstairs to get herself some cereal.

On the way to the kitchen, she stopped to plug in the tree—the one sign that Christmas was actually coming to their house.

Mom was already at the kitchen table when Martha walked in, and Martha never did get out the cereal, because Dad was making her favorite breakfast. Martha drizzled real maple syrup over her stack of three perfectly round banana pancakes. She took a bite and closed her eyes in bliss as she chewed and swallowed.

Dad made pancakes better than anyone!

Mom laughed. "Look at her, Peter!" she said.

Martha opened her eyes and watched her mother looking at her father and her father looking at her. Something big and warm swelled up and burst inside Martha's chest. She took another bite, but this time she kept her eyes open, smiling her pleasure around the table to her family. So she was gazing right into her mother's eyes when the smile dropped from her mother's face. Two small lines appeared between Mom's brows, and her hand went to her belly. Martha put down her fork. Dad was at Mom's side instantly.

"Something's happening," Mom said. "Something's not right."

"Let's get you to the couch," Dad said. "I'm calling the doctor."

Dad steered Mom out of the kitchen. In the doorway, Mom stopped and gave a small mew of pain. Like a kitten that's been stepped on, Martha thought. What was that baby doing to her mother?

"I think she's coming. The baby's coming right now," Mom said. "And she's not due for more than a month."

Mom was crying, actually crying. And every bit of the joy that Martha had felt over a stack of banana pancakes turned to fear. Even her knees and her elbows were afraid.

"All right," Dad said. "Let's go straight to the car. I'm taking you to the hospital right now."

Martha stood by the kitchen table and watched her parents forget all about her. Fear for her mother blended with a surge of panicky loneliness. They were just going to leave her there!

No.

As they passed back through the kitchen on the way to the garage, Dad turned. The look on his face scared her more than anything. He was frightened too, that look said. It only lasted a moment.

"Come, Martha," he said. "We'll drop you at Doug and Angie's."

Martha didn't even question the choice. She just grabbed her coat and went.

Mom phoned Angie from the car while Dad drove. She was still making those little mewing sounds every little while, once right when she had Angie on the phone. And Angie and Doug and Chance were waiting outside when they pulled up.

"Goodbye, sweetie. We'll call," Dad said. He turned his head and smiled a wide smile at her, and she smiled a wide smile back, but both of their smiles were thin, just lips stretched across teeth.

Mom opened her car door, called Martha to her and hugged her, pulling her as close as she could with that baby belly in the way. Martha hugged back, clinging almost. How could they leave her here?

"All right, Martha. We've got to go," Dad said, and Martha released her mother.

"Goodbye," she said to them, her lower lip wobbling.

"Goodbye," they said back to her, together. "We'll call."

She stood and watched them drive away, fingering the key in her pocket.

"Just in case," Dad had said when he handed it to her. "If I can't get back, Doug or Angie can take you home to pick up a few things."

"But you will get back. Right, Dad?" Martha had said.

"I'm sure I will, sweetheart, but just in case."

Martha did not like the sound of that. Just in case. Just in case what?

Chance's foster sister Louise toddled. She toddled and toddled and toddled. And everyone fell all over themselves in raptures about it. Everyone, that is, except Martha. Louise was fat and round all over. Her hair was fluffy and blond, like an Easter chick's feathers. She laughed a lot. She screamed a lot. She cried a lot.

Martha looked at her. My mother is at the hospital having one of those, she told herself. More than a month early, she added. Surely Mom wasn't actually going to have the baby now!

They were all at the kitchen table. Martha had a ham-and-cheese sandwich on a plate in front of her. She had managed to take one small bite out of it. Louise was in her high chair, not toddling now, but throwing bits of sandwich on the floor and smearing other bits around on her tray. Chance was coaxing her to take a bite by playing choo-choo with it. Doug and Angie's "real" son Mark was wolfing down his lunch. He was on his way out and had wanted to take his sandwich with him, but Doug had insisted he sit down and eat with them.

"We have a guest," Doug said.

"She's not *my* guest," Mark said, but he kept his eyes down and half swallowed the words, as if he didn't really want anyone to hear them.

"You will sit down at that table, and you will eat your lunch," Doug told his son.

Mark was shoving in his last bite and sliding out of his chair when Angie put a platter of cut-up fruit on the table and sat down beside Martha.

"Are you worried about your mother?" she said softly.

Martha gave a small nod. She hadn't been thinking about Mom just then, but she was worried. Yes, she was.

"She's going to be fine, you know. And one of these days—maybe even today—you're going to have a baby sister."

Martha nodded again and looked at Louise. Part of the choo-choo train had found its way into Louise's mouth, and she was gumming it, with loud smacking noises, while she pounded her fist on her tray to some rhythm all her own.

How delightful, Martha thought, screwing up her nose in disgust. She would probably be scraping dried food off the kitchen floor for years after the baby came home. She gave her head a shake. Maybe she could banish mothers and babies once and for all.

Angie put a hand on her arm and smiled into her eyes. Martha smiled back as best she could, but she didn't feel very smiley. She turned her head enough to put Louise out of her sight and took another bite of her sandwich.

What was happening at the hospital?

Lunch over, Mark out the door and Louise supposedly drifting off to sleep in her crib, Angie said, "I think we all deserve an early Christmas present. And I know just the one!" She went to the tree that towered crookedly in the living room's bay window, and pulled a rectangular package out from under it.

Martha had spent a long time looking at that tree before lunch, doing her best to think bad things about it. It was nothing like any tree she had ever had at her house. First of all, it was real. It smelled outdoorsy, and the carpet and the presents were littered with needles. Second, the ornaments didn't match, and you could tell that some of them were handmade. A Santa leered at her, his body misshapen, his mouth far too big for his face. Mark must have painted that in some long-ago year. Martha was pretty sure that this would be Chance's first Christmas with Angie and Doug.

Some of the ornaments looked very, very old. A delicate wire-and-metal ship balanced on a branch, ready to sink forever at a mere touch. Two small angels, painted onto dark brown felt, twirled gently, almost as if they were flying.

It was a beautiful tree.

The presents, though…they were a disaster. They looked as if Louise had wrapped them blindfolded. And some were wrapped in newspaper, of all things! Martha turned to the couch, where Chance was pulling the color comics off the present that Angie had selected.

A game. They were going to play a game together.

All the way from the living room, Martha could hear Louise chattering away to herself in her bed. Perhaps she would interrupt them. Or maybe, even better—much, much better—the doorbell would ring, and Dad would be there with Mom in the car, and they would go home to their artificial tree, their red-and-gold ornaments and maybe even a bright-ribboned gift or two.

Louise settled down, neither the doorbell nor the phone rang, and the four of them played their game. It was all about building roads and towns and claiming farmland, stuff like that. Martha might have liked it at another time and with other people, but not then and there, with them. Not with the telephone sitting silent on the coffee table.

She was distracted, and as Chance pulled ahead in the game, her mood worsened. At one point, when Chance got excited about completing a small town, Martha lost her temper right in front of Angie and Doug. "It's no big deal, you know," she said, her tone mean. Chance shrugged.

"We know this is a hard day for you," Angie said sweetly, "but there's no need to take it out on Chance."

"Sorry," Martha squeezed through her teeth, thinking, I could *take it out on him* a lot worse than that!

And then, at last, at long last, the phone rang. Martha jumped up but had to wait while Doug answered the phone, which was infuriating because they all knew it was for her. He looked at the call display and said, "I think it's your dad, Martha."

Filled with relief and fear together, Martha held out her hand. But he didn't even seem to see her. He just pressed *Talk* and put the phone to his own ear.

Martha stood right beside him, but he kept right on listening into the phone. "All right," he said. And "Oh dear." And "Yes, of course. She's more than welcome here. We'll take good care of her." And finally, finally, when Martha was getting set to use force, he handed over the phone.

"Hi, Dad," she said softly, walking through to the empty kitchen and trying not to think about Doug's words, *We'll take good care of her.* "When are you coming to get me?"

"I'm sorry, honey, but we're not," Dad said. "Not for a while. Your mom needs to stay in the hospital for a few days. She needs some extra special care so that the baby can come at the right time. And she needs me with her."

Martha stood up against the kitchen counter, rigid, the phone pressed hard against her ear. Need. Need. Need.

"But, Dad, you can't leave me here. You can't!" she whispered. Then, almost so quiet he wouldn't hear, "It's Christmas."

Silence at the other end for a long moment, and then two deep breaths. "I know this is hard for you, Martha, but I need you to stay strong." He paused. And Martha stood, listening, breathing, until he spoke again. "Listen, honey, I have to go. Can you pass the phone to Doug? I'll get him to take you to the house to pick up your pajamas and things."

Mute, Martha walked back into the dining room, where the game was laid out on the big table, clutter pushed aside to make space. Mute, she handed the phone over. Mute, she wandered through the big archway into the living room and sat down on the couch. Mute, she listened to Doug's end of the rest of the conversation.

She could feel Angie and Chance looking at her. Her chin gave a wobble, and she steadied it. Her will was strong.

"Yes," Doug was saying into the phone. Pause. "Yes... Yes. All right. Goodbye, Peter. Take care of yourself and Denise. It's all going to be fine. You'll see."

Another pause, a short laugh, and he hung up the phone.

"Martha," he said, his voice warm and kind.

She stared at the tree, wishing she could jump up and kick him.

"Your mom and the baby are going to be just fine, but your mom needs to be in hospital right now, and she needs your dad with her."

Martha looked up at him from the couch. She did not say, "What about what I need?" Or, "I don't care about the baby. I just want my mom back." Or, "But it's Christmas!" She did not shout, "How can they do this to me?" Or scream, "I hate you guys!"

But she wanted to. How she wanted to!

"Get your coat, and we'll go and pack you a bag. What do you say?"

"All right," Martha said, her voice hardly more than a squeak.

CHAPTER 10

In the Finite Forest

The house, when they got there, felt as if it had been empty for years. It felt like a sad house, a lonely house. Martha charged up the stairs of the sad, lonely house, turning her head away from the row of photos as she ran.

Her small suitcase was in her closet. It only took a minute to fill it up with stuff: a flannel nightgown, slippers and a robe, some clothes, her hairbrush. She went into the bathroom and got her toothbrush. Back in her bedroom, she stopped and thought for a moment. Then, because that was what she always did when she packed for overnight, she turned to her bookshelf.

Ah.

She had started Lemony Snicket's A Series of Unfortunate Events in the spring, but thought them a bit silly. They seemed just about perfect now. She grabbed the ones she hadn't read yet, books four to eleven, laid them on top of everything else and zipped up the bag.

Done.

She paused in the doorway and thought about the carefully wrapped package she had stuffed under the bed that morning. At least she wouldn't be needing that! She wasn't going to have to share Christmas with a baby that wasn't even born.

She bit her lip hard. Sure, Angie had said her mom was going to be okay, but what if she was wrong? What if her mom was dying? Dying! And here Martha was feeling glad that she didn't have to hand over a present. Tears washed up the backs of her eyes.

When she came out of the bedroom, Doug was waiting at the bottom of the stairs. She wasn't thrilled that he had come right into her house without asking, but she didn't say a word. She just held her body as straight as she could and marched right past him,

out the door, down the walk and straight into the backseat of his rumbling, crumbling car.

Back at Doug and Angie's, Doug carried her small bag and led her upstairs. Chance was up there, standing in the hallway, arms full of stuff—a pillow, a couple of books (must be mostly pictures, Martha thought), a clear plastic bin of pencil crayons—looking up at Angie. "Why can't she sleep on the pull-out couch? That's where other guests go."

Martha was sure that he had seen her coming before he had opened his mouth. He wanted her to hear this. He wanted her to know. He didn't look at Martha, but she could still see his tight mouth and the flush on his face. Chance was mad. Really mad.

Angie just smiled, put her hands on his shoulders and steered him down the hall. He was moving in with Mark, where there were twin beds, and Martha was to have Chance's room all to herself. Angie had a bunch of clean sheets under her arm. At least Martha assumed they were clean. They didn't have that fresh, folded look that clean sheets had at her house. These looked like they had been bundled straight out of the dryer into the linen closet.

“Where’s Louise?” Doug said from the doorway of what must have been Chance’s room.

“Mark’s watching her,” Angie said. She smiled. “At least he promised to. Chance,” she called, for Chance had passed through a door with all that stuff in his arms, “can you go downstairs and help Mark keep an eye on Louise?”

Martha heard a crash from inside the room that Chance had just entered. She imagined pencil crayons skittering across the floor. Chance came into the hall with his chin down and his shoulders up. When he pounded down the stairs, Martha could have sworn the house shook. She wasn’t sure that she would trust Louise to him in that state.

“It’s hard for him to be uprooted,” was all Angie said a few minutes later as she pulled the quilt up over the wrinkly sheets that they had just put on Chance’s bed.

Hard for Chance! He had found the perfect home at last. He was part of a family. They were probably going to adopt him any second. He was about to spend Christmas with them. He should be doing somersaults down the hall, not stomping down the stairs!

But, no. He was too spoiled to let a girl whose mother might die, who was practically an orphan, spend one single night in his house.

Well, she knew the best treatment for that. She was not afraid of a silly little boy. Martha followed Angie downstairs a few minutes later. They went through the dining room, and Martha glanced at the game, abandoned on the table. Would Angie and Doug want them to finish it?

No, they would not be finishing that game. All the pieces were askew. Strewn on purpose, Martha was sure. The television blared some cartoon from across the hall. In a moment of bewilderment, Martha pictured her mother in a hospital bed. She was screaming. No. She was white and still. Martha shoved the awful pictures out of her head.

Desperate, she darted into the kitchen. "Can I help with supper?" she said.

Supper was strange. Apparently it was what these people always ate the night before Christmas, but it didn't seem very festive to Martha. Some sort of thick, gloppy thing with hunks of meat in it, served with powdery boiled potatoes. Mark gulped his down, chattering away about his afternoon as he ate. Mouth empty. Mouth full. It seemed to make no difference to him. Or to anybody else.

The rest hardly spoke. On Martha's left, Chance tapped his fork on the edge of his plate, rhythmless and relentless. Martha had heard the expression "attention-seeking behavior." Well, wasn't that tapping just a classic (and annoying) example? Mark reached out and snatched at Chance's hand several times and appealed to his parents once.

"If he needs to tap, let him tap," Doug said.

"Tap, tap, tap!" Louise shouted, grinning around a mouthful of potatoes.

Martha spent the dinner hour imagining that her body was divided precisely down the middle. Her right side was normal; her left, a perfect sculpture carved in ice. She sat straight, shoulders back, and angled her body toward the dining companions who were worthy of her attention.

She never looked at that boy, not even for one second, even though the tapping made her want to snap her fork in half with her teeth. And he never said one word. Not even one. So she did not have the satisfaction of learning how the chill affected him. Still, she enjoyed the exercise.

Dessert was just ice cream, vanilla or chocolate. If Angie couldn't bake, couldn't she at least scan the shelves in the grocery store?

"Time for the movie!" Angie said as she spooned up the last melted bits in her bowl.

"Ohhh, I was going to go online," Mark said.

"Not on Christmas Eve. That's family time. And I'll bet that Chance has never seen *It's a Wonderful Life*!"

Martha would have bet all the money in her beaded purse that Mark wanted to say, *Let Chance watch it then*. But he didn't. Angie went off to put Louise to bed. Doug started washing the pots while Mark, with only a bit of grumbling, loaded the dishwasher with dishes that Chance carried out to him. Martha did look at Chance then, but he didn't look back at her. He still seemed stiff and angry, his eyes fixed mostly on the ground. He had a lot of nerve!

Her frozen left side was melting by the minute, and misery was leaking into her bones. She couldn't stand there waiting patiently and then sit and watch some movie about a wonderful life. She couldn't!

"I'm going upstairs," she said, though she was pretty sure only Chance could hear, and he made no sign.

In Chance's room, Martha unzipped her suitcase to get her nightgown, and there were the Lemony Snicket books right on top. She gathered them up and put them in a stack by the bed. Then she sat down, just for a moment, opened *Book the Fourth* and scanned the first couple of pages. *The Baudelaire orphans looked out the grimy window of the train and gazed at the gloomy blackness of the Finite Forest, wondering if their lives would ever get any better.*

Forget a wonderful life. This was more like it! Moments later, dirty clothes in a heap on top of the open suitcase, teeth unbrushed, hair uncombed, she was in that wrinkly bed, burrowing her way into a book for the first time since she had learned that her mother was going to have a baby. Halfway through *Book the Fifth,* she fell asleep with the light on.

CHAPTER 11

Mom Calls

The banging on her door woke her, and for a moment Martha didn't know where she was.

"You have to get up!"

Martha had been fast asleep, and she was pretty sure that she had been having a great dream. Goodbye to that. She managed to hold her eyes shut tight for only another moment before the banging came again and the voice. This time the door flew open. That brought her eyes open and her feet onto the floor.

"Hey! You can't just barge in!"

"I can so. It's my room." Chance was positively vibrating. "You have to come right now. We're not even allowed to touch our stockings till everyone's down there." The words were ground out between his teeth and spat bruised and bloodied into the room.

If she had been the type, Martha would have been frightened. As it was, she moved away from him along the side of the bed.

Through the open door, Martha saw Mark walk past on his way downstairs. He glanced in at them. "Come on, Chance," he said.

Then Angie and Doug and Louise were there. All of them. Louise waddled in, her face alight with excitement even though she had no idea what Christmas was all about. Her wet diaper hung down almost to her knees. Martha edged a little farther away.

"Merry Christmas," Angie and Doug said, together, but not quite. Their faces were alight too, but they were watching her a little bit too carefully. They didn't seem to be aware of the state their foster son was in.

"Merry Christmas," she mumbled as she watched them back. Then she got it. Pity. Pity was all mixed in with those smiles. And that pity felt like a big scratchy rock right inside her heart. "All right, all right," she said. "I'm coming." And she managed a smile, just to get them all out of the room.

Chance ran past them, and by the sound of it, hardly touched down on the stairs.

Again tears threatened. One even got out and onto her face. It was bad enough having to cope with this weird place, but when she remembered why she was here, she could not bear it. She dug in her suitcase for some clean clothes. She wasn't going to sit around downstairs in her robe and slippers. She just wasn't.

Angie's voice floated up the stairs. "Martha, are you coming?"

The living room looked just like a storybook. The tree was lit up, the floor beneath it heaped with presents, their sloppy wrapping lit invitingly by the multicolored lights. Doug was on his knees laying a fire in the fireplace—a real fire!—and, above his head, six fat, lumpy stockings hung all in row. Angie was handing out hot chocolate. And music was playing. "Hark, the Herald Angels Sing."

Mark was on the couch distracting Louise, who looked more normal and less smelly in a clean diaper.

Chance, though...Chance was pacing the room when she came in, but he stopped dead when he saw her. Dead. She took a step backward. She hadn't taken *such* a long time upstairs. Had she?

Doug leaned back on his heels and held out an arm. "Chance," he said, "come here." The voice was calm and insistent, and Chance went. Martha felt him pull his eyes off her, as if they were sticky tape on her skin, maybe sticky tape with tiny knives built in. On his way to Doug, he kicked the corner of the couch. Hard.

"Hey!" Mark said.

Angie handed Martha a mug and ushered her to the couch. Then she went to the far side of the fireplace and began to take down the stockings.

Doug had Chance in the crook of his arm now and was speaking quietly into his ear. When Chance replied, it was not so quiet. "I have to be nice to her at school. On field trips. Trick or treating. Everywhere. And now I have to give her my room. And she's nasty and stuck-up. She won't even come downstairs when she's supposed to." He stopped for a moment, and when he spoke again, his voice was higher, louder. "She's wrecking everything. I don't want her here. I don't!"

Doug spoke some more into his ear.

"But it's Christmas." Again a pause, longer this time. "My first real one."

Martha got up from the couch. She felt her body straighten, almost robot-like, and her voice, when it came out was precise, prim. Yes, that was the word. Maybe she had one of those dolls' mechanical voice boxes in her throat.

"I'm sorry," she said. "I don't want to ruin anyone's Christmas."

Chance had turned again when she started to speak, and there were his eyes again, stabbing into her skin.

"I didn't ask to come here. I didn't ask for any of this!" Now she was shouting and crying all together. "It's Christmas for me too!" Even in her miserable state, she hated the way she lengthened the word *too*, whining and crying all at once.

Angie put down the stockings and pulled Martha against her. Doug was on his feet. He stood behind Chance, hands on his shoulders.

Martha heard Mark speak under his breath. "Great. Just great!" he said.

"Christmas is hard for a lot of people," Angie said. "Martha, you miss your family, and you're worried about your mom. Chance, this is your first Christmas with us, and you've been looking forward to it, and now Martha is here. All right. You've both expressed your feelings. We sympathize."

Martha couldn't see behind her, but she'd bet Angie gave Mark a look at that point.

"Now we are going to open our stockings together and drink our hot chocolate. Then we are going to have breakfast."

They seated Chance and Martha on opposite sides of the room. Martha stared at her feet, trying to stop the tears from coming. She had never been so humiliated in all of her life. She jumped when something was laid in her lap. A stocking. She blinked. It was her stocking from home! She looked up, and Doug was smiling at her.

"Your dad told me where it was," he said. "And I snuck in and found it. They wanted you to have your own stocking on Christmas."

That brought the tears back. It must have been hanging by the fireplace when she came in. She hadn't even taken in that six stockings meant one for her, let alone that it was her very own. She unhooked the candy cane from the top.

Strange, though. The stocking *was* hers. The beautiful needlepoint snowy woodland scene had greeted her on every Christmas morning that she could remember. But the contents seemed wrong. A package wrapped in yellow tissue paper stuck out the top. The paper had been kind of crushed around the gift and encircled with scotch tape to keep it there. Her stocking always contained gifts neatly wrapped in thick embossed or patterned paper.

It took some doing to get that yellow paper off. Inside was a book. Not new. *The Secret Garden* it was called. She looked inside. *For Angie, with love from Auntie Flora* it said. Underneath that was a note to her: *For Martha, a special book for a special girl, with love from Angie.* She flipped farther on: *When Mary Lennox was sent to Misselthwaite Manor to live with her uncle, everybody said she was the most disagreeable-looking child ever seen. It was true too.* Martha must have gasped out loud, because she heard a laugh from across the room.

"You're beautiful inside and out, Martha, not disagreeable. But I think that you might like that book. I did when I was your age." Angie paused. "And I still do. I think it's almost time for me to read it again!"

Martha managed a small smile and set the book aside. The rest of the stocking was surprising too. And, unlike at her house, nothing but the book was wrapped. First was a small stuffed monkey, its skinny arms wrapped and pinned around a fat marzipan pig. Martha wasn't sure that she liked marzipan, but she liked the monkey. He had a bright smiling face that pleased her. Next came some sort of puzzle made up of a stack of squares of cardboard with parts of a picture on them that you had to match up to each other. Under that was a box of pencil crayons and a small pad of thick drawing paper. And near the bottom, a bag of licorice and a packet of round syrupy, sandwichy-looking things called *stroopwafel*. She could feel another lump down there, near the bottom, that was round but not an orange. Martha reached her arm down, way down, and closed her fingers around a smooth sphere. She pulled it out, and the light struck the thin glass instantly, sparkling off the gold-painted pattern: a Christmas ornament. Martha held it up and gazed at it as it spun gently on the end of its golden thread.

Again, Angie was watching her. "You can hang it on the tree here if you like. That way you'll be able to enjoy it until it's time to go home. Then you can take it with you."

Martha shifted her stocking and its contents onto the couch beside her, got up and walked over to the tree. Music flowed over her. The fire crackled. The tree smelled of pine. And she saw the perfect empty spot just at eye level near a yellow light. It took a moment to get the glittery ball to hang so that it could swing without hitting any branches, but she did it and then stood back.

"It looks perfect," Doug said.

Martha nodded. Yes. It *was* perfect!

She turned back to the room and found herself face-to-face with Chance.

She looked into those hurt, angry eyes and, once again, the magic of the morning was gone. She was in a strange place with strange people, one of whom hated her. Hated her! It was Christmas morning. And her life was never, ever going to be the same again.

A silent cry rose from deep inside her. It didn't come out, but it filled her from the middle, right out to the skin of her front and her back and her scalp and the soles of her feet. Martha wanted her mother—not the sick woman in the hospital with a baby inside her, a baby that had already managed to ruin her life. No. She wanted her proper mother back. The one who made snacks and entertained her friends.

And loved only her and her dad.

She stood in the middle of the room. Helpless. And Chance stood looking at her, hurt and wanting to hurt back. Anyone could see that. He had emptied his stocking. She could see the contents over on the floor where he had been sitting. She looked at him again, and this time she saw what he held in his hands.

"Go on, Chance," Angie said. "Hang your ornament on the tree too!"

Martha could have told them they shouldn't give a mere visitor exactly the same thing they gave their foster son on his very first Christmas with them. It seemed like a no-brainer to her.

He kind of bundled his glass ball onto the tree—setting it on a branch instead of hanging it by its thread—and retreated.

Angie scrambled to her feet. "Let me help you," she said. And she hung the glittery ball so that it twisted and turned and caught the light.

Breakfast followed. A quiet breakfast. Pancakes—nowhere near as good as Dad's—and sausages and mandarin oranges. Chance gulped his down and left the table. Martha ate hers almost as fast, excused herself and headed back to the living room to collect her stocking, her book and the other things. Chance was sitting on the floor by his stocking, holding a small glass-and-metal butterfly. A strange present for a boy, Martha thought as she stuffed her gifts back into her stocking. Then she remembered the painted lady butterflies from last year's class. No one had loved those creatures as much as Chance, though he'd been pretty weird about it.

He did not seem to notice Martha. She climbed the stairs and closed her door behind her. She did not want to think about her mother. She did not want to think about that boy. *Book the Fifth* was there on the bed, but a certain disagreeable-looking child was calling to her, drowning out the voices of the Baudelaires. She opened *The Secret Garden* at page one.

Hours passed before the tap on her door. Doug this time, on his own. He had a small wrapped gift in his hand. A small gift wrapped in silver embossed paper and tied with thick shining ribbon. Martha scrambled up to sit on the bed, her insides melting into mush as she did so. She took the package from Doug and looked up at him, waiting for him to go. He sat down beside her.

She began to untie the ribbon, taking care, as her mother always did, and buying time, as she needed to at this moment. She didn't want to cry in front of Doug. Putting the ribbon aside, she started on the paper. Doug shifted beside her.

"You don't have to stay," she said, surprised at how normal her voice sounded.

"I want to," he replied. "Your dad asked me to tell you something about it once you've opened it.

It was a camera. A small pale green camera. It could shoot video too. And it was gorgeous. Martha felt a small rush of the old familiar Christmas excitement. Mixed with relief. They loved her. They had thought of her. They had got something special just for her.

She started working away at the cellophane wrapping on the box.

"Your dad said that you could bring it to the hospital when the baby's born. You can be the family photographer!" Doug said.

The box sat on her lap, and her hands grasped it lightly. The baby. Even this gift that had found its way to her in another kid's bedroom in a strange house was all about the baby. The familiar rush of warm fuzzy feelings—they all evaporated. The scratchy rock was back.

"Thanks, Doug," she said. "I'm going to read a bit more now, if that's okay." She pasted on a bright smile. "I love the book Angie gave me!"

Doug stayed seated for a moment. "All right," he said. "I could help you get that camera working this afternoon, if you like."

"Sure," Martha said, hoping he could tell that she was just being polite.

And he was gone.

This time, neither Mary Lennox nor the Baudelaire children had anything to offer her. She pushed the camera box onto the floor, turned over and curled up on her side, pulling her knees up to her chin, and stared at the wall.

And stared at the wall some more.

The problem was that when she did that her mind filled right up. There was her mother, in a hospital bed. She shoved the image away. There was Martha in the hospital snapping photo after photo of a perfect little baby wrapped all in pink. She replaced it with an image of Louise gumming her food. That helped a bit. There was her dad telling Doug where to find the stocking and the parcel. And that brought her scrambling up, back against the wall. Her chest heaved and she was sobbing. Sobbing right out loud.

They hadn't called. It was the middle of the afternoon, and they still hadn't called. Something was wrong. It had to be.

Footsteps sounded on the stairs. Martha scrubbed at her face with her hands and slid off the bed. Someone tapped on her door, and she opened it a crack. Just a crack. And peered out. She snatched the phone from the hand, barely even noticing whose hand it was, and pushed the door shut.

"Dad?" she said into the receiver, eager, breathless, frightened—no—terrified.

"Sweetheart, it's me!" a voice said. "Merry Christmas!"

For the longest moment, Martha had no idea who was speaking to her.

"You'll never guess where I am," the voice went on. "Maui!"

Linda. It was Linda. Martha held the phone away and looked at it, trying to understand. The voice kept right on coming at her, even across the space. She put the phone back to her ear.

"Brad surprised me yesterday. He had the tickets. We flew down here last night. Your dad gave me the number to call to reach you. And guess what? We're getting married today. Today!"

A pause. At last Linda seemed to notice Martha's silence. "Martha, are you there?"

"Merry Christmas, Linda," Martha said numbly, "and congratulations."

"I don't know what I'm going to wear. I mean, I did bring a dress, but it's not really a wedding dress. And it's so warm here. Do you think I should go shopping?"

"Sure," Martha said. *What do I care?* she thought.

"You know, now that we're going to be married, Brad wants to start a family right away—" Linda broke off, and Martha heard her suck in a big breath. "Oh, honey, your dad told me Denise is in the hospital. I'm so sorry. Is she going to be all right? And the baby—"

It was wrong. It was just wrong, and Martha wasn't going to allow it anymore. Not for one more second.

"My *mom*," she said. "She's *my mom*. Not Denise. I have to go now. Have a nice wedding." And with no assistance from her, Martha's finger reached out and pressed the Off button. She put the receiver back to her ear.

Dial tone. Martha remembered the bag with Linda's gift back at the house. Oh, well.

CHAPTER 12

Crows at Sunset

She didn't even have time to sit back down on the bed before the phone rang again. She stared at it, grasped in her hand. What would she say? How would she explain hanging up like that?

She pressed the Talk button. "Hello," she said.

"Hi there," Dad said.

Tears just flew out of her eyes. "Hi," she replied, hoping that her voice didn't sound too wobbly.

"Merry Christmas, sweetheart. I'm so sorry that you have to be there all by yourself."

The tears settled down right away to a steady flow. "Merry Christmas, Dad," Martha replied. "It's okay. How...how's Mom?"

Was that a pause? Did Dad's voice just sound worried? Or was he scared too?

"Well, Martha. It looks like your sister is going to be born right on Christmas Day! Your mom's going in for a Caesarean in an hour."

"A Caesarean?"

"It's a special procedure to take the baby out."

Martha couldn't quite absorb what he was telling her. And she didn't like the word *procedure*! Then her father shocked her.

"She's right here, and she wants to say hello."

For the tiniest second, Martha thought he meant the baby!

And then a different voice was speaking to her.

"Merry Christmas, Martha," Mom said.

For a long moment Martha couldn't speak, she was crying so hard. She drew in a breath and heard sniffling through the phone. Mom was crying too.

Why was Mom crying?

"Are you…Are you going to be okay?" Martha said and wanted to bite back the words.

"I'm going to be fine, Martha. Just fine."

Dad's voice replaced Mom's, and Martha sucked back her tears. Nothing about this conversation felt "just fine."

"Honey, is Doug there, or Angie?" Dad said.

Martha made her way downstairs to the kitchen and put the phone into Doug's hand. She did not stay to listen to what was said.

In the living room, the lights sparkled on the tree, and her golden ball and Chance's silver one spun when she touched them. The smell of roasting turkey filled the house. Martha wasn't sure if that smell was comforting or not. She wandered to the window and pulled aside the curtain, which was already drawn at four in the afternoon.

She stood, the curtain still in her hand, and stared. The sky was brilliant orange, almost the color of a Christmas mandarin, and the river below the house was deep in mist.

She looked around the room. Empty. Doug and Angie were in the kitchen. She could hear the murmur of Doug's voice, still talking into the phone. Louise must be napping. And the boys just weren't there.

Martha walked—bold, daring—straight to the front door, grabbed her coat from the hook, shoved her feet in her shoes and left the house. She knew that if she asked anyone, they would tell her that she couldn't go down to the river alone. They would keep her at home or offer to come with her. "You know the rules," Doug had said. "Stay with the group."

Well, Martha was tired of rules. She did not want to be with any group, not now, not them. The mist was calling her to the river. The mist and the stillness. And the orange bits of sky.

As she came to the path along the river's edge, she gazed out into the mist and saw lumps floating everywhere. Lumps that became sleeping ducks when she looked a second time. She set off along the trail. People who passed her looked about for her adult, but Martha didn't care. She was old enough and big enough and confident enough that no one said a word. She walked on. She had planned to explore the quay, but a mist-shrouded couple was already there, so she kept to the shore.

The mist had cleared a bit close by, or perhaps she had walked out of it, for she saw a pale blue canoe tied up to a log below the quay, and she saw the water now, dead calm, like glass, like a mirror. Its orange surface drove her gaze upward to the sky, which was a place in itself, all clouds and color. Then she heard the cawing. She looked higher still.

Crows. A murder of them. She loved that they were called that, a murder. She had learned it after her encounter with the hungry crow at the Discovery Center. They were crossing the river, high, high in the sky, passing right over her head. They were going home, back to the woods near Boundary Road. That was what Doug had told her that day. They were coastal crows, and they used to live way far west near the beaches. Now they lived right in between Vancouver and Burnaby. Thousands and thousands of them. As she watched, the crows above her flew on, at least a hundred of them. She looked back the way they had come. And saw more. Many, many more. All coming from the same place. All flying in the same direction, streaming for their roosts.

She fixed her gaze on the far side of the river behind the last of the crows. Moments passed. Then black specks appeared, as if someone had sprinkled pepper on the sky. The specks turned into more crows, approaching across the water. She watched. Another forty specks. Then another.

"What are you watching?"

Martha turned, startled and angry all in an instant. It was Doug.

"Crows," she said.

He looked blank.

She sighed. "There," she said, pointing at the bank of clouds on the far side of the river. "Watch."

Moments later, they gasped together.

"At sunset," Doug said, "the crows go home to roost."

Martha ignored him.

She was determined to see them all, every last one.

He didn't seem to mind.

During a time when the sky was empty, she gazed sideways at her unwelcome companion. "See the ducks?" she said.

He looked where they floated, heads tucked, far from shore, in the middle of the sunset. The river blazed as orange as the sky.

"The river is so calm," he said. "They feel safe out there."

"Maybe they like the mist," Martha said.

"Maybe they do."

Man and girl looked back to the sky. Empty.

"Time to go home," Doug said. "Angie is worried. And so is Chance."

Martha scoffed. She had never really known what *scoff* meant until that moment. Now she did. It meant the way her whole face and body contracted against what Doug was saying.

Chance was not worried. Maybe…maybe Angie was. But not Chance.

He was out in the street, waiting for them as they climbed the hill.

"You can't just go off like that!" he shouted as they approached.

Martha strode right past him, trying to hide her heavy breathing. It was a very steep hill. Doug huffed and puffed behind her. Chance followed Martha up the steps and into the house.

"You can't! You know you can't."

Mark was setting the dining table.

"Come on, Chance. Let up on her," Mark said. "Hey, Martha, what were you doing out there? Mom and Dad were really worried."

Martha was already marching up the stairs. "Your mother and father do not have to worry about me," she said. The next minute, she had closed her (Chance's) door behind her and was stretching out on the narrow bed, letting herself drift. Crows and ducks. An orange sky.

She started awake. How much time had passed? Would her mother be having that "procedure," whatever it was called, right now? Right this minute?

Crows. Crows and ducks. An orange sky.

What were the crows saying to each other, high above her? Maybe she could get someone to take her to see those crows roosting one night. Then, in her mind, something big moved beneath the water. Something old. A sturgeon. A sturgeon swam beneath those sleeping ducks without waking a single one. She remembered the diving bird. It had seen the sturgeon. She was sure of it. She could almost feel the fish as it swam by, smooth and cool and wet against her skin. She shivered.

And jumped as a sharp knock sounded on her door.

Angie and Doug had come together. Martha had to sit up straight on the bed and face them. Did no one around here wait to be invited in?

In her mind, the sturgeon sank back into the mud. The crows settled into faraway trees. The ducks pulled their heads from beneath their wings and paddled off to find a more peaceful sleeping spot.

With them gone, her mother and her "procedure" pushed their way in.

Martha gave her head a shake, trying to draw comfort from the heavy shift of her hair. She knew why Angie and Doug were there, and she knew what she was supposed to say.

"I shouldn't have gone off like that." She raised her eyes and opened them wide, trying to look really, really sorry. She liked the idea of Doug and Angie gazing into her eyes and marvelling at the depth of her regret.

"You're right, Martha. You shouldn't. We know you're worried about your mother and the baby."

Martha shook her head at them hard. Don't talk about Mom. Don't talk about Mom.

"But that doesn't mean that you can do dangerous things. You're only nine years old. We're responsible for you. And you didn't even tell us you were going. If Doug hadn't seen you at the bottom of the hill, we might have called the police."

Martha stared. The police? Were they crazy?

"All right," Doug said. "That's enough for now. I smell turkey!"

The rest of Christmas all fit into one small moment for Martha. It came while she was choking down a tiny serving of that delicious-smelling turkey.

The phone rang. Her fork clattered onto the table, and her chair almost tipped right over as she jumped up. This time they let her answer the phone herself.

"Dad?" she said.

"Ten fingers. Ten toes." He oozed joy into the phone. The huge ball of fear inside Martha cracked open.

"Mom?"

"Your mom's fine, honey. Just fine. They're both sleeping now."

Martha held the receiver in both hands. It turned out that balls of fear were full of salty water, and all that water had to come out. She didn't have any words. All she had were tears. Maybe a million tears.

"I'm coming to get you on my way home," Dad said. "And we'll visit them together in the morning." He paused. "Okay?"

Martha could manage that. "Okay," she said, while the tears kept right on coming.

CHAPTER 13

New Baby

Martha knew that she should be excited. She had been last night, when Dad came to get her. She had lain awake for a long time, happy to be in her own bed, excited about seeing her mom. Surely now everything would be all right.

But in the morning, at breakfast, it all changed.

"Adrienne has the biggest eyes," Dad said. "I'm sure she stared right at me yesterday, even though they say babies can't see that far."

"Mmhmm," Martha said. She tried to imagine this tiny new baby with her big eyes.

Adrienne?

"You named her?"

"It's was my mother's name. Your grandmother's."

Martha had never met any of her grandparents. They had all died before she was born. "Who was I named after?" she asked, even though she knew the answer.

Dad looked at her. "Linda chose your name, Martha. You know that."

Why did you let her? Martha thought. Why did *she* get to name me?

Dad got up and carried their bowls to the sink. "I love your name, Martha," he said. "And you're named after your aunt Serena too. Also a beautiful name! Now let's get a move on. Your mom can't wait to see you!"

Martha was wondering why Serena was her middle name, not her first, when he added, "Do you have your camera?"

She swallowed hard and went to get it. She had brought the camera home still in the box, but Dad had asked for it right away and set it up for her, chattering the whole time about photographing that baby sister of hers.

All the way to the hospital, Dad went right on chattering. He described Adrienne. He said that Mom could come home in a day or two and Adrienne might be ready to come home in a week or ten days. She was in a special room and a special bed called an isolette because she had been born early. She needed to be in a place where she couldn't catch any diseases, and she needed a little bit of help with her breathing.

Help with breathing? That caught Martha's attention. It sounded scary.

"Will I be allowed to hold her?" Martha asked, though she was not at all sure she wanted to.

"Not right away, honey," Dad said. "Like I said, she's in a special room. And no children under twelve can go in. There is a window out to the hallway. You can see her through that."

So Martha would not be allowed near the baby sister that she had never wanted. The car was a quiet place for a while, with Dad looking at her over his shoulder every minute or so. Then he took a breath and started talking about how much help Mom was going to need.

Martha stared out the window, thinking about Cinderella. If they had a real fireplace in their house, like Angie and Doug, she could curl up on the hearth at night with a blanket and put breakfast on the table with her hair done up in a kerchief and soot on the end of her nose.

It was no surprise to her that she didn't like the hospital.

She didn't like the big fake Christmas tree in the entrance hall or the tinny version of "Rudolph the Red-Nosed Reindeer" that drifted through the halls.

She didn't like the people. In the elevator, two doctors talked openly about their patients like a banker might talk about money or a grocer about lettuce.

Sick people wandered the halls, some pushing metal poles with clear plastic bags hung on them. Sick people huddled outside, beyond the protected no-smoking area, sucking on cigarettes. (Cancer sticks, Dad called them.) Visitors slumped on benches, looked aimlessly at all the useless stuff in the gift shop or clutched ugly flowers on their way to someone's room.

She didn't like the way the place smelled.

Everything in the hospital felt clean but not clean. Otherwise, why would there be all those bottles of hand sanitizer everywhere? Martha squeezed some into her hands before she got onto the elevator and again when she got off. She wasn't taking any chances.

The maternity ward was different from the rest of the hospital. There, life began. No one was sick. And everyone was happy.

Everyone except Martha.

Martha knew that she had been in a maternity ward once before. Most people had, after all. And Mom had told her the story, like, a million times. Mom and Dad had been so happy. Linda had been so glad to have a wonderful home for her baby. Martha had been such a beautiful baby.

Martha had seen pictures, and she knew that the last bit was an out-and-out lie.

She was pretty sure that other parts of the story were lies too.

Her bag felt heavy on her shoulder. It held that hastily wrapped present. She had been so sure about the present when she had woken up with the brilliant idea on Christmas Eve. She felt much less sure now. She wasn't even sure that she wanted to give any of them any presents at all. Still, she had brought the package along. Dad had not appeared to notice.

Dad had stopped outside a door.

"Here we are!" he said and let Martha step past him into the room.

There was only one bed in the room. The head of the bed was raised, and Mom was half sitting up. Her head was tilted to the side against the pillow, and she was asleep with her mouth open. The blanket only came up to her waist. Martha averted her eyes from the stains on the nightgown. She knew they had to do with feeding the baby, and she didn't like them. Dad walked past her and leaned over to her mom, one hand laid gently on her shoulder. Martha went and stared out the window at the parking lot.

"Martha?" Mom's voice said.

Martha turned, and there was her mother smiling at her. She had pulled the sheet up over her chest, smoothed out her hair and closed her mouth.

Gulping back her relief, Martha crossed the room in a moment. She leaned across the bed to hug her mother and was surprised when Mom shrank away. Dad's hands on Martha's arms pulled her back.

"Not like that," he said from behind her. "Your mom's a bit delicate at the moment. She has stitches in her tummy."

Mom reached up and grasped her shoulders. "I'm fine up at the top," she said. "Give me a kiss."

But Martha was afraid now. She had only ever had stitches once, in a finger. She kissed her mother on the cheek without touching her anywhere else.

Mom didn't seem to notice.

It felt awkward just standing there, so Martha reached for the package she had set down by the door. She had to get Dad to hold the bag while she wiggled it out.

"What's that?" Mom said.

Martha didn't say anything. She just put the parcel on Mom's legs, well away from her stomach.

Both parents looked at her. She nodded toward it. Didn't they know what to do with a present? Dad stepped forward and untied the ribbon. Moments later, the stack of books was revealed. They looked kind of old and uninteresting, Martha thought. Still, an impulse made her reach into her pocket for her new camera.

Mom reached for *When We Were Very Young*. "My favorite," she said and opened it. She found Martha's inscription right away.

Martha had written *For all four of us. To share. Merry Christmas.* She had put the year at the top so they would always remember this was the baby's first Christmas.

Mom smiled, and Martha snapped a picture. She noticed that Mom's eyes were wet.

"Why did we ever put this away, Martha?" Mom said. "I know just which one I want to read first."

Several more long moments passed before she put the book aside and looked up at them. "I think it's time," she said then. "Help me into the wheelchair, Peter, and let's go see her. Martha, you can watch through the window. Can you lend us your camera?"

Step by step, Martha followed them down the hall and stationed herself outside a big picture window that looked into a room filled with machines, the Intensive Care Nursery. The ICN. She had to search for a moment to identify the isolettes, the small clear boxes, at counter height, with tubes running in and out. One of them looked empty, but in the other two she could make out what must be babies.

Dad and Mom appeared in the room, looking strange in gowns and masks. He wheeled her up to one of the isolettes and whipped out the camera. For the next ten minutes, Martha watched through the glass, alone. She watched Mom struggle to her feet and the two of them gaze at the small creature in the glass box. Martha couldn't help but think of Snow White. After a while, she saw them step back and look around, obviously upset by something. A nurse came. Mom sat back down and the nurse took the baby from the isolette and placed her in Mom's arms. From where she stood, Martha could hear the baby's cries, muted by glass, and she could see the tension in Mom's body.

Martha didn't notice that Dad had left Mom's side until he showed up at hers.

"She doesn't seem so tiny when she cries," he said, and Martha swam suddenly back into herself. "And five pounds isn't bad at thirty-five weeks," he added. "Look. I made a video for you."

In the video, Adrienne was sleeping. Martha stared. She had not expected five pounds to look quite so tiny. Premature: a preemie, they called her. Dad had zoomed right in on her face and Martha could see her mouth smacking a little and her eyelids twitching as she slept. Her face was pink, pink, pink. Then the picture zoomed out. Adrienne was wearing a tiny pale pink cap and a white sleeper covered in pink bunnies and yellow chicks, so only her face and her hands showed—two teeny-tiny, scrunched-up hands. Clear plastic tubes ran into her nose.

Over Martha's shoulder, Dad gazed adoringly at the screen. "She's waking up now," he said.

Martha stared as the baby's face went from pink, pink, pink to red, red, red. Her mouth opened wide, and her eyes squeezed tight shut. Her cheeks looked like little red apples, and Martha thought of Snow White once again, though she was pretty sure Snow White would cry much more prettily.

She was amazed at the sound that such a small creature could make, faint though it was filtered through the little camera.

"Look at them now," Dad said, and Martha raised her eyes from the camera to the window.

In the nursery, Mom was holding the baby close. The baby had to be sleeping, because Mom looked so peaceful.

"They might rest together for a while," Dad said. "We'll leave them to it. Let's go see what we can find to eat. "

The cafeteria was thoroughly decorated for the season. Dad got gingerbread boys and hot chocolate for both of them, and they sat near a window overlooking the street. Martha watched the video again while she nibbled at her cookie. Several questions bubbled up inside her, but she let them drift away unasked. Wasn't it awful to be cut open to get the baby out? Was Mom going to heal up all right? Was the baby going to be okay? At last Martha thought of a question she felt safe enough to ask. "When can I see her properly?" she asked. "The baby...Adrienne, I mean."

"Soon, I hope," Dad said.

And Martha found that she hoped so too.

As it turned out, three days passed before things changed, before Adrienne was breathing mostly on her own. She was still in the special nursery and still in an isolette with a breathing tube, but she was getting stronger by the hour, the nurses said. They could make an exception and allow Martha in, because the other preemie had gone home.

For a long moment Martha hovered in the nursery doorway before she followed Mom—on her own two feet now—and Dad into the room. She had never worn a mask and gown and gloves before. She felt awkward and alien, not like herself at all.

Adrienne was asleep. Martha stood and watched her chest rise and fall, rise and fall. That chest contained lungs, she thought, and a heart. So small.

"Would you like to hold her?" Mom said.

Martha was not at all sure about that, but Dad guided her to the big beige plastic-covered chair. She tried to settle herself inside and out, but before she had a chance to stop her own heart from racing, the nurse was handing her the baby, putting Adrienne right into Martha's arms.

"Support her head," Dad said.

As he said it, Martha felt the head wobble, all floppy on Adrienne's skinny neck as it kind of slid off Martha's arm. She put her other hand under it, but that was awkward, and she didn't like it, a whole head with a brain inside and everything, almost fitting right into her hand like a softball. The baby squirmed, and her eyes opened. The blanket she was wrapped in came loose, and her arms and legs flailed. Then her eyes screwed up and her mouth opened, and the quiet was shattered. Any trace of wonder that remained in Martha was wiped away by that terrible screaming. What was wrong? Had she hurt her somehow?

"Please, Dad. Take her," Martha said.

The nurse did not come this time, and it seemed to take Dad forever to get Adrienne quiet and back into her isolette. By the end of it, Martha was exhausted.

She longed to go home, to her nice quiet bed and her book.

"I got a picture," Dad said when all was quiet again, "before the screaming."

Martha looked at it in the car on the way home. Dad had caught her cupping Adrienne's head in her hand, before the slipping blanket and the flailing limbs. Martha was surprised at the beauty of Adrienne's face and by the hint of a smile on her own.

Maybe having a baby sister would not be a complete disaster after all.

CHAPTER 14

Home

The next week passed in a blur. Adrienne came home halfway through it, and home did not feel like home anymore.

First of all, baby stuff was spread absolutely everywhere. Second, Mom was exhausted. So was Dad. There were no proper meals. Angie had offered to come over every Friday to clean the house. That was good, because otherwise, the filth would have piled up forever. The thing of it was, Angie expected Martha to help.

And in between, Martha had to load gunky dishes into the dishwasher, turn it on when it was full, and put all the dishes away when it was done, chipping off dried-on guck with her thumbnail. She was tired of canned soup and baked beans and neon orange macaroni and cheese. She tried to make herself a grilled cheese sandwich one day, and Dad came running into the kitchen thinking the house was on fire. First he shouted at her. Then he told her in his pretend-calm voice that nine was too young to use the stove all by herself.

She was lucky they let her use the microwave. Otherwise, she would probably starve.

The first time Angie came over, she brought Chance.

It was obvious that he didn't want to come. It was equally obvious that all the adults had talked. They had planned. Martha and Chance were supposed to make up.

Martha led Chance into the TV room and put on a movie. They sat at opposite ends of the couch and stared at the screen.

It was a funny movie. About halfway through, they both laughed at the same moment. Martha turned her head and found Chance looking right at her.

"So now we both have babies in the house," Chance said.

Martha hesitated. Then she said, "Yeah."

And silence fell between them again.

"I kind of lost it when you were at my house," Chance said in the middle of a car chase.

Martha hesitated again. She guessed that was supposed to be an apology. And, in that moment, she found that she wanted to put the bad feelings behind her. Chance might be a bit strange. He might struggle at school in lots of way. But he was kind of interesting. He cared about stuff like butterflies and fish. She wondered what he thought about crows.

"That's okay," she said at last. "I know what it's like to be invaded." And she nodded toward the baby stuff all over the floor.

When the movie was finished, they went into the kitchen to find some lunch.

The holidays were almost over, and Mom still seemed so different. Her face was pale and extra wrinkly, and she had dark poochy bags under her eyes. Her stomach still stuck out under her grubby oversized T-shirt, even though Adrienne had been out of that stomach for almost two weeks now. She had to push herself up out of chairs with her arms—sometimes Dad or Martha helped—and she walked kind of like an old person, biting back groans once in a while. But she also seemed more relaxed in a funny way. She wasn't always "getting things done" now. She sat with the baby and let mornings and afternoons and evenings slide by. She talked and she listened. Martha read aloud from her Christmas present to them and from Angie's Christmas present to her, and Mom let her go on for ages.

Sometimes Martha would hold Adrienne while Mom read to them instead. Martha loved that even more, now that she knew how to keep Adrienne's head from wobbling. She would listen while something big and warm filled her chest as she gazed down at that tiny perfect face.

It was turning out to be kind of all right, this baby thing.

On the last night before school started again, Martha remembered Linda's present. She brought the bag down to the living room, where Mom was stretched out on the couch and Dad was sitting with Adrienne in the big chair.

Martha sat down on the carpet. She reached into the bag and pulled out a small square object wrapped in green tissue. "Linda gave me this when I saw her," she said in response to their surprised looks. "I forgot all about it."

Mom struggled into a sitting position. "I wondered about that," she said. "I figured she must have changed her mind about giving it to you."

Martha felt a little twist in the region of her heart. She set the small package down. Mom already knew all about it.

"Open it, honey," Mom said. "She just checked with me to be sure it was all right with us. She wants to be part of your life, but she doesn't want to interfere."

Martha sat perfectly still and tried to absorb what Mom had just told her. It made Linda seem different. More thoughtful. More caring. Less desperate. She picked up the parcel and tore off the paper.

Inside was a jewelry box, an old-fashioned one, black and velvety, the kind that snaps open and shut. It took her a moment to bring herself to open it.

Please, please, please let me like what's inside, she said to herself. And when at last the box lay open in her palm, she found that she did.

It held earrings, one pair. A single pearl dangled from each thin gold shepherd's hook. Looking closely, she could see that one of the pearls was worn down a bit. She looked up at her mom.

"Linda's mother gave them to her not long before she died. Linda was only eight at the time, and she wore them all the time for years. That's why they are so worn. She wanted you to have something that connects you to your mother and your grandmother in your birth family. I told her I thought you would love them." Mom paused and gazed at Martha. She took a breath. "You don't have to wear them though."

"Oh, I want to," Martha said, "definitely!" And she got up and went to the bathroom to put them on.

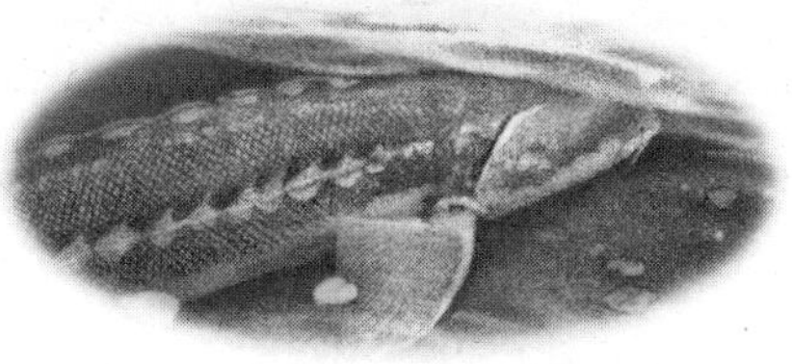

CHAPTER 15

School Again

It felt good to go back to school after the Christmas break. Doug and Chance showed up on foot at Martha's house at eight thirty that first day. Chance and Martha were to walk together for now, since Mom had to stay with the baby and Dad was going into work late, so as to be home with the baby too.

Here was one more proof, Martha had tried to tell herself. Now that they had their own baby, they didn't need her anymore. It felt great to discover that she didn't believe a word of it.

Showing up with Chance chattering away at her was a bit embarrassing, but if anyone could pull it off, she could. She sent off her brightest beams of confidence as they entered the school.

They turned into the hallway outside their own classroom and stopped. An enormous sturgeon covered the wall, all the way from their door to the next. The fish gleamed with silver paint mixed in with the brownish gray. The one eye they could see looked out at them a little sadly, as if the creature wished that it could twitch its tail and trade the dry echoing hallway for the muddy depths of the Fraser River.

"We did good," Chance said. And he beamed.

Martha had never approved of beaming. She didn't approve of the expression "did good" either.

But she looked into his beaming face. Her own cheekbones pulled up toward her eyes. Chance stared. He beamed some more. And Martha knew, without a mirror to look into, with no one to consult, that she was beaming right back.

"Yeah," she said. "We did."

Martha straightened her shoulders. She had been waiting all morning for Preeti to separate herself from the others. Many months ago, Mom had suggested that Martha call the girls to explain why she had rushed them out of the house. Martha had refused. Well, over the last eight months, her own stubbornness had tired her right out.

The moment had arrived. Sam and Hailey were picking up Sam's lunch from the office. Preeti was at the back table painting the scutes on her sturgeon, which was almost ready to join Martha and Chance's in the hall. Chance was back there too, but that was all right.

Martha put a hand on her hip. The purple and gray skirt was just right. She was pretty sure no one could see where she had washed baby spit-up off her shirt.

The walk to that table seemed long. Then came the moment when she stood over Preeti, lips and tongue frozen, while Preeti gazed up at her. That seemed longer. At last, Martha spoke. "So, my mom had her baby," she said, letting out her breath in a long slow stream along with the words.

Preeti blinked. "She did?" she said.

"Yeah," Martha went on, "it's a girl. I have a baby sister."

"Hmmm," Preeti said.

The announcement didn't seem to be enough. Martha squirmed. The classroom door opened, and Sam and Hailey burst into the room. Martha almost bolted for her desk.

Almost, but not quite. She breathed deeply as the two other girls approached. A second deep breath, and she was able to form the words. "I'm sorry I was so rude to you that day," she said. "That was the day my mom found out she was pregnant." She paused and looked at them, desperate. "Anyway, I shouldn't have acted like that."

"It was weird," Hailey said.

"And mean," Sam added.

Silence fell.

On the other side of the table, Chance smiled as he cut another round brown sturgeon egg out of construction paper.

"What's your sister's name?" Preeti asked.

"Adrienne," Martha replied. "My sister's name is Adrienne."

Acknowledgments

Thanks to my friend and editor, Sarah Harvey, for all her guidance, especially her assistance with my prickly character, Martha. And thanks to Teresa Bubela, for making this book so beautiful, and to everyone else at Orca for all that you do.

Maggie de Vries is the author of seven books for children, including the picturebooks *Tale of a Great White Fish: a Sturgeon Story* and *Fraser Bear: a Cub's Life,* and the prequel to this story, *Chance and the Butterfly.* She lives in Vancouver on the banks of the Fraser River, and in recent years has grown increasingly fascinated by the fish that swim in the river and the birds that fly above it. Maggie also teaches creative writing at UBC and UNBC, travels regularly to lead writing workshops with children and teachers, and occasionally edits children's books.